R D

MIDNIGHT NEVER COMES

JACK HIGGINS

OPEN ROAD

INTEGRATED MEDIA

NEW YORK

Copyright © 1966 by Jack Higgins

ISBN: 978-1-4532-0014-8

Published in 2010 by Open Road Integrated Media
180 Varick St.
New York, NY 10014
www.openroadmedia.com

CONTENTS

CHAPTER ONE

Last Chance

THE MOMENT HE PUSHED OPEN THE door and paused on the edge of darkness, Chavasse knew that he had made a bad mistake. Somewhere deep inside, a primitive instinct, that slightly mystical element common to all ancient races and inherited from his Breton ancestors, combined with the experience that came from ten hard years of working for the Bureau and touched him coldly, sending a wave of greyness moving through him.

As he took a hesitant step forward, the darkness was filled with a hideous, frightening clamour and a red light flashed on above his head reaching into the four corners of the small room.

Jorgensen was standing by the window, immaculate in the beautifully-cut dinner jacket he had worn earlier, the rose still fresh in his lapel. He stood there, legs slightly apart, a .38 Smith & Wesson magnum in his right hand, barrel pointing to the floor.

Chavasse slid a hand inside his jacket, reaching for the Walther automatic in its special pocket, knowing he hadn't a chance and Jorgensen grinned almost apologetically.

'Too late, Paul. About a thousand years too late.'

As the red light went out, he fired and the flash picked him out of the darkness for one brief second, the last thing Chavasse saw before the heavy bullet smashed into him just below the breastbone, lifting him off his feet and back through the open door into the corridor.

He hit the wall hard and slid to the floor, struggling for air, aware of voices near at hand, of running feet in the darkness and then the corridor light came on and Jorgensen appeared in the doorway.

Chavasse still held the Walther in his right hand. He started to raise it and Jorgensen stood there waiting, the Smith & Wesson held against his thigh, something close to pity on his face. The Walther fired, the bullet kicking plaster from the wall at least three feet to one side of him, then it seemed to jump out of Chavasse's hand. He gave a strange choking cry and pitched forward on to his face.

Hammond went up the curving Regency staircase and passed along the corridor. It was strangely quiet up there, somehow remote and cut off from the world outside, the only sound the slight persistent hum from the dynamos in the main radio room. He mounted two steps into another corridor, opened a large white-painted door and went in.

The room was small and plainly furnished, lined with green filing cabinets, its only occupant the woman who sat at the desk by the far door typing busily on an electric machine. She was perhaps thirty, plump and rather attractive in spite of the heavy library spectacles she wore. She stopped typing and looked up anxiously.

'Have you heard?' Hammond said.

She nodded. 'How is he?'

'He didn't look too good when I left. They've got him in the medical room now.'

She nodded at the canvas grip he was carrying. 'Is that what he was wearing?'

Hammond nodded. 'Yes, the Chief wanted to see it. Is he in?'

She flicked the switch on the intercom and the dry, remote voice joined them at once. 'What is it?'

'Colonel Hammond is here, Mr. Mallory.'

'Send him in.'

Hammond moved to the door, opened it and went in. He closed it softly behind him and waited. The man who sat at the desk reading a sheaf of typewritten documents by the light of a shaded desk lamp might have been any high Civil Service executive at first glance. Everything about him seemed part of a familiar pattern. The well-cut dark-blue suit that could only have come from Savile Row, the Old Etonian tie, the silvering hair. And then he glanced up and Hammond was aware of the sudden shock that contact with those cold grey eyes always gave and that strange irrational feeling that he was once again a young subaltern fresh out of Sandhurst, meeting his commanding officer for the first time.

'Let's have a look at it then.'

Hammond moved forward quickly, opened the canvas grip and took out a sleeveless jerkin whose nylon surface gleamed in the lamplight.

'This is the bullet-proof waistcoat he was wearing?' Mallory asked.

'That's right, sir. Manufactured by the Wilkinson Sword Co. I believe they prefer to refer to them as flexible body armour.'

Mallory weighed it in his two hands. 'It's heavier than I had imagined.'

'Sixteen pounds. Nylon and titanium. Capable of stopping a .44 magnum bullet at point-blank range.'

'Was that what Paul was hit with?'

Hammond shook his head. 'Smith & Wesson .38.'

'And he's all right?'

'Badly winded. He'll have a nasty bruise for a week or two, but that's all.'

'I understand he lost consciousness.'

Hammond nodded gravely. 'I'm afraid so. If you want my honest opinion, I'd say he was in a pretty poor state of health generally and his nerves seem shot to pieces. Jorgensen said he didn't think he'd last five minutes in the field.'

Mallory gave a sudden exclamation of anger and jumped to his feet. He lit a cigarette, moved to the window and stood staring out into the night.

'It can happen to the best of us, sir,' Hammond said. 'And from what I've been told, he did rather ask for it. I understand this Albanian affair he got mixed up in wasn't even official business.'

Mallory nodded. 'That's true, although the outcome was important from our point of view.'

'What happened, sir?'

'I sent Chavasse to Albania last year to make contact with what's left of the Freedom Party there. He had a rough time. Only just got out by the skin of his teeth so I gave him some leave. We had a girl working in our S2 organisation in Rome—a Francesca Minetti. Italian father, Albanian mother. She persuaded Chavasse and a friend of his to run her across to Albania from a small Italian port called Matano. Her story isn't important now, but Chavasse fell for it.'

'He must have been mad.'

'No reason to doubt her. She'd worked for the Bureau for several years remember. I appointed her myself. She took us all in.'

'A double agent, presumably?'

'That's right. The whole thing was simply a rather clever ruse to enable the Albanians to get their hands on Chavasse and it nearly succeeded.'

'What happened to the girl?'

'Oh, she got what was coming to her, but not before she'd stuck a knife into Paul. Nearly finished him off. In fact you could say that she's succeeded in the final analysis.'

'Was there an enquiry?'

Mallory shook his head. 'No, we can put our own house in order. There won't be any more Francesca Minettis, I can promise you that.' He sighed heavily and dropped the end of his cigarette into the ashtray on the desk. 'Pity about Chavasse though. The most successful agent this department has employed in the fifteen years I've been in charge. I'd even nourished some kind of vague hope that he might survive long enough to take my place when it's time for me to go.'

'I'm sorry, sir,' Hammond said, 'I hadn't realised that.'

Mallory moved across to the sideboard and poured himself a whisky. 'I first came across him in 1955. He was a university lecturer at that time—Ph.D. in modern languages. A friend of his had a sister who'd married a Czech. After the war her husband died. She wanted to return to England but the Communists wouldn't let her go.'

'So Chavasse decided to get her out?'

Mallory walked back to his desk. 'The Government couldn't help and as Chavasse spoke the language, he decided to do something unofficially.'

'It must have been difficult, especially for an amateur.'

'How he managed I'll never know, but he did. He was in hospital in Vienna recuperating from a slight injury when I decided to have a look at him. Perhaps the most interesting thing about him was what he calls his language kink. You know how some people can work out cube roots in their heads and others never forget anything they've ever read? Well, Chavasse has the same sort of gift for languages. Soaks them up like a sponge—no effort.'

'So he joined the Bureau?'

'Not right away. At first he wasn't interested. He went back to his university post the following term. It was during the Christmas vacation that he came to see if my offer was still open.'

'Did he say why he'd changed his mind?'

'He didn't need to.' Mallory took a Turkish cigarette from an ivory box and inserted it carefully into a jade holder, his one affectation. 'Paul Chavasse has everything a good agent needs. Flair, ingenuity, a superb intelligence plus common sense—and those two don't always go together. Added to these he has the willingness to kill, something most human beings hesitate over, even in a difficult situation.'

'So he decided he wanted a more active life?'

'Something like that. I think the Czechoslovakian affair had made him discover things about himself that he never knew before. That he liked taking a calculated risk and pitting his wits against the opposition. Teaching French and German in a red-brick university must have seemed pretty tame after that.'

'And this was what—ten years ago?'

Mallory nodded. 'I'll tell you one thing, Hammond. I'll be lucky to replace him.'

There was a discreet knock on the door and Jean Frazer came in with a large buff envelope which she placed on the desk. 'The medical reports on Paul Chavasse, Mr. Mallory. The Medical Room says they'll be sending him up in about fifteen minutes.'

Mallory looked down at the envelope and sighed. 'All right, I'll see him as soon as he arrives.' She turned to the door and he added softly: 'And, Miss Frazer. I don't want us to be disturbed—not on any account. Is that understood?'

She went out and Hammond got to his feet. 'Anything more I can do, sir?'

Mallory shook his head. 'This is my baby, Hammond. I'll see you in the morning.'

The door closed and a small trapped wind whistled softly around the room and died in a corner. Mallory looked down at the envelope, remembering many things and pulled himself up hard. That sort of sentimentality never did anyone any good. He put on his spectacles, took out the medical reports and started working through them.

Chavasse lay on his back on the operating table and stared up at his image multiplied again and again in the reflectors on the low ceiling. The bruise was already beginning to show beneath his breastbone, dark with blood, but he could feel no pain.

The very flesh on his body seemed to have shrunk, emphasising the ugly puckered scar of the old gunshot wound in his left shoulder, and the great angry weal of the knife scar that had gutted him like a herring from just above his hip to a point an inch or two below his left nipple.

Ten years. Ten hard, bloody years and this was all he had to show for it. He pushed himself up and as he swung his legs to the floor, the door opened and Dr. Lovatt came in, pipe clamped firmly between his teeth. He ran one hand through the untidy shock of white hair that fell across his forehead and grinned.

'How do you feel, Paul?'

'Terrible. My mouth's like a sandpit.'

Lovatt nodded. 'I gave you a quarter grain of morphine to kill the pain.'

'That's a little old fashioned, isn't it?'

'Still nothing like it as far as I'm concerned,' Lovatt said. 'I'm not going to change my ways just because some drug company sends me a flashy prospectus.'

He leaned forward to examine the knife scar, tracing its course gently with the end of a finger and Chavasse said calmly, 'What do you think?'

'Time, Paul. That's all it needs.'

Chavasse laughed harshly. 'Why pretend? It's taken the sap out of me and you know it. Have you finished the tests?'

'We have. You can get dressed.'

'And what's the verdict?'

'Mallory's got the reports now. He'll see you as soon as you're ready.'

'It's like that, is it?'

'A long rest, that's all you need, but he'll have all that in hand I'm sure.' He moved quickly to the door before Chavasse could reply. 'I'll probably see you again before you go.'

Chavasse dressed slowly, a slight frown on his face. The tests hadn't gone too well, he was certain of that, especially the ones which had followed the fiasco with Jorgensen, but what would the Chief do, that was the point? Put him out to pasture for two or three months perhaps and then give him a job on the inside? It would be nice to be in from the field for a while, or would it?

He was too tired to think straight and the morphia was really beginning to take effect so that he even found difficulty in knotting his tie properly. The Walther automatic was lying on the table together with his wallet and loose change. He weighed it in his hand for a moment, frowning, then slipped it into its special pocket inside his jacket and left. When he went out into the corridor, the building seemed unnaturally quiet and he glanced at his watch. Half-ten. They'd all be away now except for the Duty Officer and the night-shift men in the radio room.

But he was wrong for when he opened the door to Mallory's outer office, Jean Frazer was sitting at her desk. She removed her spectacles, got to her feet and came to meet him, concern on her face.

'How are you, Paul?'

He held her hands briefly. 'Never felt better, Jean. Is he in?'

She nodded and tightened her grip as he started to pull away. 'I thought you might like to come back to my place afterwards. You look as if you could use a decent meal. We could talk things over. It might help.'

For a moment, his face was illuminated by a smile of great natural charm so that he might almost have been a completely different person. He touched her cheek gently and there was real affection in his voice when he spoke.

'Don't waste your time trying to put the pieces together again, Jean. They just won't fit any longer.'

Something seemed to go out of her and her shoulders sagged. Chavasse turned away, tapped once on Mallory's door, opened it and went in.

Mallory sat at his desk, the medical reports before him, cigarette smoke drifting up through the light of the shaded lamp. He glanced up, his face sombre and nodded briefly.

'You don't look too good, Paul. Better sit down.' He got to his feet. 'How about a drink? Whisky suit you?'

'Not according to my doctor,' Chavasse said. 'Or haven't you read those reports yet.'

Mallory hesitated, leaning on the desk with both hands. 'Yes, I've read them.'

'Then could we kindly get this over with. It's been a hard day.'

Mallory took a deep breath and nodded slowly. 'All right, Paul, if that's the way you want it.'

He sat down and opened the file in front of him. When he spoke again, his voice was brisk and formal. 'I'm afraid your fitness tests have proved negative.'

'All of them?' Chavasse said. 'I certainly don't do things by halves, do I?'

'You never did,' Mallory observed dryly. 'Frankly, you would seem to be in a pretty low state of health generally. Understandable, I suppose, in view of what you went through in Albania and then the knife wound didn't help. Dr. Lovatt tells me it's had to be opened up and drained on three separate occasions.

'Something like that. He seems to think a nice long rest in the sun is indicated. What can you offer?'

Mallory removed his spectacles and leaned back in his chair. 'The fact is that I've nothing to offer you at all, not any more. You see, the psychiatrist's report didn't make any better reading than this little lot. It seems your nerves are shot to pieces. He even thinks you need treatment.'

'At ten guineas a time he would,' Chavasse said. 'You must be joking. He couldn't psychoanalyse his way out of a wet paper bag.'

Mallory straightened in his chair and slammed a hand hard down on the desk. 'For God's sake, Paul, face facts. What about your practical earlier this evening? You went in after Jorgensen like an amateur. In the field, you'd have been dead, don't you understand that?'

'I understand only one thing,' Chavasse said bitterly. 'That I'm being slung out on my ear. That about sums it up, doesn't it?'

'No one asked you to get mixed up in that Albanian affair,' Mallory said angrily. 'You went in of your own accord.'

'Believing in the word of a member of this organisation,' Chavasse said. 'Someone you appointed yourself, so I understand.'

There was a moment of heavy dangerous silence as they challenged each other across the desk and then Mallory sat down heavily. When he spoke, he was completely in control again.

'You'll get the usual pension, Paul, we owe you that at least.' He opened a red file and took out a letter. 'I've been in touch with an old friend of mine, Hans Muller. He has the chair in Modern Languages at one of the new universities in the Midlands. He'll be glad to have you on his staff.'

Chavasse laughed once and it had an ugly sound. He pushed back his chair and got to his feet. 'It's been fun, Mr. Mallory. As our American friends say, a real ball.'

He started for the door and Mallory jumped to his feet. 'For God's sake, Paul, don't be a fool.'

Chavasse paused, one hand on the door knob and grinned crookedly. 'I remember reading somewhere once about a French abbé who'd come through the revolution. Someone asked him what he'd done during the Terror. "I survived," he said. "I survived." I suppose I could say the same. Something to be grateful for at least.'

He opened the door quickly before Mallory could reply and went out.

CHAPTER TWO

THE MAN WHO
HAD CH'I

SOMEWHERE IN THE DISTANCE BIG BEN struck midnight, the sound curiously muffled by the fog and then there was silence. It was raining heavily and Chavasse paused on a corner to button the collar of his trenchcoat up around his neck.

Since leaving Jean Frazer's flat, he had walked aimlessly, turning from one street into another until he had come to the river again. He wasn't too sure where he was, probably Wapping from the look of it. Not that it mattered very much. He walked across the road past towering warehouses and paused beneath a street lamp, leaning on the stone parapet above the river.

He unbuttoned his coat, sliding his hand inside searching for his cigarette case and his fingers touched the butt of the Walther. He pulled it out and examined it quickly, a slight frown on his face. Technically speaking he would be committing an offence from now on simply by continuing to keep it without a permit.

He held it out over the dark water for a moment and then changed his mind and slipped it back into its pocket. When he found his cigarette case, it was empty and he continued along the wet pavement, turning the corner into an old square surrounded by decaying Georgian houses.

There was a Chinese restaurant on the other side, a ten-foot dragon in red neon glittering through the rain and he crossed towards it, opened the door and went in.

It was a long, rather narrow room obviously constructed from the ground floor of the house with the internal walls taken out. It was scrupulously clean and decorated in a vaguely Eastern manner, probably to please the clientele.

There was only one customer, a Chinese of at least sixty with a bald head and round, enigmatic face. He couldn't have been more than five feet in height, but was incredibly fat and, in spite of his immaculate tan gaberdine suit, bore a distinct resemblance to a small bronze statue of Buddha which stood in a niche at the back of the room, an incense candle burning before it. He was consuming a large plate of chopped raw fish and vegetables with the aid of a very Western fork and ignored Chavasse completely.

The Chinese girl behind the bar had a flower in her dark hair and wore a *cheongsam* in heavy black silk brocade embroidered with a red dragon that was twin to the one outside.

'I'm sorry, sir, we close at midnight.'

'Any chance of a quick drink?'

'I'm afraid we only have a table licence.'

She was very beautiful. Her skin had that creamy look peculiar to Asian women and her lips an extra fullness that gave her a distinctly sensual air. For some strange reason Chavasse felt like reaching out to touch her. He took a grip on himself, started to turn away and then the red dragon seemed to come alive, writhing across the dark dress like some living thing and the walls moved in on him. He lurched against the bar and was aware of her voice faintly in his ear.

Once in the Aegean, diving from a sponge boat off Kyros he had run out of air at sixty feet and, surfacing, had experienced that same sensation of drifting up from the dark places into light, struggling to draw air into tortured lungs.

The fat man was at his side, supporting him effortlessly with a grip of surprising strength. Chavasse sank into a chair. Again, there was that strange sensation of not being able to draw enough air into his lungs. He took several deep breaths and managed a smile.

'Sorry about this. I've been ill for rather a long time. I haven't been up for long. Probably walked too far.'

The expression on the fat man's face didn't alter and the woman said quickly in Chinese. 'All right, uncle, I'll handle this. Finish your meal.'

'Do you think they will come now?' the fat man said.

She shrugged. 'I don't know. I'll leave the door open for a little while longer. We will see.' The fat man moved away and she smiled down at Chavasse. 'You must excuse my uncle. He speaks little English.'

'That's all right. If I could just sit here for a minute.'

'Coffee?' the girl said. 'Black coffee and perhaps a double brandy?'

'Just try me.'

She went behind the bar and took down a bottle of brandy and a glass. At that moment a car drew up outside. She paused, frowning slightly, and peered through the window. Steps sounded on the pavement. She turned and nodded quickly to the fat man.

'They are here,' she said simply in Chinese.

As she came round the end of the bar the door opened and four men entered. The leader was at least six feet tall with a hard raw-boned face and restless blue eyes. He wore a three-quarter length car coat in cavalry twill, the fur collar pulled up around his neck.

He grinned pleasantly. 'Here we are again then,' he said in a soft Irish voice. 'Got it ready for me, dear?'

'You are wasting your time, Mr. McGuire,' the girl said. 'There is nothing for you here.'

His three companions were typical young layabouts dressed in the height of current fashion, hair carefully curled over their collars. One of them was an albino with transparent eyelashes that gave him an unpleasant, tainted look.

'Now don't give us any trouble, darlin',' he said. 'We've been good to you. Twenty quid a week for a place like this? I think you're getting off lightly.'

She shook her head. 'Not one penny.'

McGuire sighed heavily and plucked the bottle of brandy from her hand in a sudden quick gesture, tossing it over his shoulder to splinter the mirror at the back of the bar.

'That's just for an opener,' he said. 'Now you, Terry.'

The albino struck like a snake, his hand clawing at the high collar of the silken dress, ripping it savagely to the waist, baring one perfect honey-coloured breast. He pulled her close, cupping the breast in one hand and giggled.

'It's lucky for you I'm not that kind of boy, darlin'.'

The fat man was already on his feet and Chavasse kicked a chair across to block his way. 'Stay out of this, uncle,' he said quickly in Chinese.

In the moment of astonished silence which followed, the four men turned quickly to face him. McGuire was still smiling. 'What have we got here, then, a hero?'

'Let her go,' Chavasse said and the voice seemed to come from somewhere outside him so that he had difficulty in recognising it as his own.

The albino giggled and when he bared his teeth, they seemed very white against the full red lips and something snapped inside Chavasse, rising up into his throat like bile, threatening to choke him. It was as if all the frustrations of the day, all the pain and anger of six months of ill-health, of hospitals and endless operations had been waiting for this moment to explode in one white hot spasm of anger.

He pulled out the Walther and fired blindly, shattering another section of the mirror behind the bar. 'I said let her go!'

The albino sent the girl staggering across the room with a quick shove, his face turning the colour of his hair. 'Look at his hand,' he said in a whisper. 'It's shaking all over the place. Let's get out of here for Christ's sake.'

McGuire had stopped smiling, but there was no fear on his face. He stood there, hands thrust deep into his pockets, his eyes never leaving Chavasse who was trembling so violently that he had difficulty in holding the gun steady.

'Just stay where you are, all of you,' he said. 'I wouldn't like to guarantee what might happen if this thing goes off again.' He nodded to McGuire. 'You— throw your wallet across here.'

McGuire didn't even hesitate. He pulled out his wallet and tossed it on to the table. Chavasse picked it up with his left hand and opened it. It was stuffed with notes.

'How much is there here?'

'A couple of centuries,' McGuire said calmly. 'Maybe a little more.'

'That should take care of the damage. Anything over can go to the widows and orphans.' Chavasse glanced across at the woman and said in Chinese, 'Do you want the police in on this?'

She shook her head. 'No—no police.'

The kitchen door had opened behind her and two waiters and a cook stood there, all Chinese. The waiters were armed with carving knives and the cook carried a meat cleaver.

'You better get out while you still can,' Chavasse told McGuire. 'You made a bad mistake. These people have their own ways of dealing with scum like you.'

McGuire smiled pleasantly. 'I'll remember you, friend.' He nodded to the others and went out quickly. The door banged behind them and a moment later, the car drove rapidly away across the square. Chavasse put the Walther back in his pocket and leaned on the table, all strength going out of him in a long sigh. He looked up at the girl and grinned tiredly.

'I think I could do with that brandy now if it's all right with you.'

And she was angry, that was the strange thing about it. She turned on her heel and pushed past the waiters into the kitchen. Chavasse glanced at the fat man, eyebrows raised.

'What did I do wrong?'

'It is nothing,' the fat man said. 'She is upset. But please—your brandy.'

He went behind the bar, found a fresh bottle and two glasses and came back to the table. 'You spoke to me in Cantonese. You have visited my country often?'

'You could say that,' Chavasse said. 'Mainly Hong Kong.'

'But this is fascinating. I am myself from Hong Kong and so is my niece.' He held out his hand. 'My name is Yuan Tao.'

'Paul Chavasse.' He took the glass of brandy that Yuan Tao held out to him. 'Presumably that bunch have been here before?'

'I understand so although I only flew in yesterday myself. I believe they have been pressing their demands here and elsewhere for some weeks now.'

The two waiters and the cook had disappeared and now the girl returned, wearing ski pants and a Norwegian sweater. She still looked angry and her cheeks were touched with colour.

She ignored her uncle and glared at Chavasse. 'Who are you? What do you want here?'

Yuan Tao cut in, his voice sharp with authority. 'This is no way to speak, girl. We owe Mr. Chavasse a great deal.'

'We owe him nothing. He has ruined everything.' She was really very angry indeed. 'Is it just a coincidence that he walks in here at such a moment?'

'Strangely enough it was just that,' Chavasse said mildly. 'Life's full of them.'

'And what kind of man carries a gun in London?' she demanded. 'Only another criminal.'

'Would a criminal have asked you if you wished for the police?' Yuan Tao said.

Chavasse was tired and there was a slight ache somewhere behind his right eye. He swallowed the rest of his brandy and put the glass down firmly. 'It's been fun, but I think I'd better be going.'

The girl had opened her mouth to speak again and paused, her eyes widening in astonishment. He ignored her and grinned at Yuan Tao. 'Give my love to Hong Kong.'

He crossed to the door, opened it and was outside before either of them could reply. He buttoned his coat and a gust of wind kicked rain into his face in an oddly menacing manner as he moved into the night across the square. The girl's attitude didn't matter—nothing mattered any more. Already, what had happened at the restaurant seemed like some strange dream, elusive, unreal.

He was tired—God, how he was tired and the pavement seemed to move beneath his feet as he turned the corner and found himself in a street that ran parallel to the Thames, iron railings on one side, gaunt shuttered warehouses on the other.

He moved across and stood at the railings, staring into the fog and somewhere a foghorn sounded as a ship moved down into the Pool. He heard nothing and yet some instinct made him turn. He was too late. An arm slid across his neck, tightening like a band of steel, momentarily cutting off his supply of air. The albino appeared in front of him, his face a dirty yellow mask in the light of the street lamp. Chavasse was aware of the man's hands moving over his body, and he stepped back holding the Walther.

'Here we are again then, darlin', he said and something glowed deep in his eyes.

A black saloon pulled in at the kerb. Chavasse acted. His left foot swung up sharply catching the albino on the right hand. He gave a cry of pain and the Walther soared through the railings and disappeared into the darkness of the river. In the same moment, Chavasse jerked his head back giving the man who held him a sharp blow across the bridge of the nose. The man gave a cry of pain, releasing his hold and Chavasse stumbled around the rear of the saloon and ran for his life.

He plunged into the fog, his feet splashing in the rain-filled gutter and there was a cry of rage behind him. A moment later he heard the engine of the saloon start up.

He could taste blood in his mouth and his heart was pounding and then he turned a corner and found himself faced with high iron gates leading on to a deserted wharf and secured by a chain and padlock.

As he turned, the car braked to a halt a yard or two away and they all seemed to come out together. The one in the lead carried a short iron bar and as he swung Chavasse ducked and the bar clanged against the gate. A foot caught him in the side and he lost his balance.

He rolled desperately over to avoid the swinging kicks and then he was jerked to his feet, two of them pinning his arms securely, ramming his back against the gate.

McGuire stood at the side of the saloon with the albino, lighting a cigarette. He shook his head. 'You asked for this, friend, you really did. Okay, Terry, slice him up good.'

The albino stopped smiling. His hand came out of the pocket of his raincoat holding an old fashioned cut-throat razor. He opened it slowly and as he started forward, saliva dribbled from the corner of his mouth.

The blade of the razor flashed dully in the light of the lamp above the gate and somewhere a cry echoed flatly on the damp air, a strange, frightening sound, shattering the night with the force of a physical blow. The albino swung round and Yuan Tao walked out of the rain into the light.

He wore no coat and the jacket of the expensive gaberdine suit was soaked by the heavy rain and somehow, he seemed different. This was no ordinary man. Chavasse knew that in an instant. And that strange cry—he had heard it before somewhere or something very much like it. The fighting shout common to all Asian martial arts from *karate* to *kendo*.

McGuire laughed harshly. 'Put him out of his misery, Charlie, for Christ's sake.'

The man with the iron bar released Chavasse. He darted round the car and ran at Yuan Tao, the bar swinging down viciously. The Chinaman actually took the blow on his left forearm with no apparent ill-effect. In the same moment, his right fist moved in a short forward jab that was unlike any boxing stroke Chavasse had ever seen. It landed high on his assailant's cheek, the bone splintered and the man spun round and fell on his face.

McGuire gave a growl of rage. He went round the car on the run and kicked Yuan Tao squarely in the stomach with all his force. What happened then would have seemed unbelievable if Chavasse hadn't seen it with his own eyes. The Irishman seemed to rebound backwards and amazingly, Yuan Tao moved in after him. As McGuire straightened, the little Chinaman hit him twice and the Irishman catapulted over the bonnet of the car and sprawled on his back moaning.

Yuan Tao moved round the car slowly, the same calm expression on his face, and the man who still held Chavasse gave a sudden cry of fear, released his grip and took to his heels.

The albino giggled horribly and held out the razor in front of him. 'Come on, fatty, let's be having you,' he said.

'What about me then, Terry?' Chavasse said and as the albino swung round, he put every last ounce of strength he had into one beautiful back-handed chop with the edge of his hand that caught him across the side of the neck.

The albino writhed in agony on the pavement and Chavasse hung on to the railings to stop himself falling down. Beyond the car, a shooting brake had turned the corner and the two waiters and the cook from the restaurant were already walking towards the dock gates, bringing the fourth man with them.

'I'd tell them to leave him in one piece if I were you,' Chavasse said to Yuan Tao. 'You'll need him to drive this little lot away.'

'A good point,' the fat man said. 'Are you all right?'

'Only just,' Chavasse grinned. 'I don't know what it was you used just now, but I'm beginning to understand why your niece was annoyed with me at the restaurant. Presumably you were just waiting for McGuire and his boys to show up.'

Yuan Tao smiled. 'I have flown in specially from Hong Kong just for that pleasure, my friend. Su-yin cabled for my help the moment these pigs first introduced themselves. I do not think they will bother us again although I intend to stay for a month or two to make sure.'

'I should imagine they'll take the point.'

By this time the three Chinese had arrived with the fourth man. Yuan Tao spoke to them rapidly in a low voice and then returned to Chavasse. 'And now we can leave. They will deal with things here. Su-yin is waiting in her car.'

Chavasse was aware of a strange feeling of elation. It was as if he had come alive again for the first time in months. As they approached the shooting brake, Su-yin got out and came to meet them.

She ignored her uncle and looked searchingly at Chavasse. 'You are all right?'

'Nothing that a drink and a hot bath won't cure.'

She put a hand on his arm. 'I am sorry for what I said earlier.'

'Nothing to be sorry about.'

At that moment a scream echoed through the rain. She turned to Yuan Tao, a frown on her face. 'What was that?'

'The little worm, the one with white hair. I was not pleased with the way he insulted you. I told them to cut off his right ear.'

Su-yin's face didn't alter. 'I see.' She smiled at Chavasse. 'We will go now. Conversation can come later.'

'If you have studied *judo* or *karate* at all, you will have heard of *kiai,* the power that makes a man perform apparent miracles of strength and force. Only the greatest of masters may acquire this and only after many years of discipline, both mental and physical.'

Yuan Tao squatted against the wall of the tiled bathroom dressed in an old terry towelling robe and peered through the steam at Chavasse who half-floated, submerged to his neck in water so hot that sweat broke from his face in great drops.

He nodded. 'Once in Japan I was taken to meet a master of *ninjutsu,* an old man of eighty, a Zen priest as a matter of fact. He had arms like sticks and weighed perhaps eight stone. The man who took me was a *judo* black belt and in a demonstration, he repeatedly attacked the old man who remained seated.'

'What happened?'

'Incredible as it may seem, the old man threw him effortlessly. He told me later that the power sprang from the seat of reflex control, what they called the *tanden* or second brain. Apparently the development of this faculty had nothing to do with physical exercising, but had been the result of many years spent in fasting and meditation.'

'That is true. All this is but a Japanese development of the ancient Chinese art of Shaolin Temple Boxing. We are told that it first came from India with Zen Buddhism in the sixth century and was developed by the monks of Shaolin Temple in Honan Province.'

'A martial art for priests surely?'

'A necessary accomplishment in those wild times. We have a saying in my province. A prudent man avoids warfare only by being prepared for it. In my own family the art has been handed down from father to son for seven centuries. There are many schools, many methods, but without *ch'i* they are all nothing.'

Chavasse frowned. '*Ch'i?*'

'*Ch'i* is the power which you in your Western world might term intrinsic energy. When it is accumulated in the *tan t'ien,* a point just below the navel, it has an elemental force, an energy which in application, is infinitely greater than physical strength alone.'

'Let me get this straight,' Chavasse said. 'Are you saying that when you strike, it isn't the weight of the blow which causes the damage, it's this inner energy.'

'Precisely. The fist is simply a focussing agent. There is no need for the tremendous punches used by your Western boxers. I strike, often from only a few inches away, punching against the internal organs, screwing my fist slightly on impact. This way one may rupture the liver or spleen with ease or break bones.'

Remembering the crunch of bone breaking back there on the wharf, Chavasse shuddered. 'Having seen it in action, I can believe you. But McGuire kicked you in the stomach with all his force and you were not affected. How do you explain that?'

Yuan Tao laughed gently. 'Practice, my friend. Forty years of practice.'

'I'm afraid I haven't got that long,' Chavasse said, getting to his feet.

Yuan Tao stood up and passed him a towel. 'One may accomplish a great deal in a month or two with discipline and application.'

Chavasse paused, the towel bunched in his hands. 'Are you saying you would be willing to teach me?'

Yuan Tao looked at him critically. 'You have been ill, my friend, your ribs show. The big scar—it was a knife, I am right?'

Chavasse nodded. 'It poisoned my whole system. I was in and out of hospital for months.'

'Forgive me, but I must ask this. The scars on your body, the gun you carried, speak of no ordinary man.'

'Until this evening I was employed by my country's intelligence service.'

'And now?'

'Pensioned off. They don't think I'm up to it any more.'

'And you would like to prove them wrong?'

He took another robe from behind the door and Chavasse pulled it on. 'I'd like to be a man again. I'd like to be able to sleep through the night, go for a walk without feeling like a broken down old hack after quarter of a mile and take a drink without being sick after it. That would be enough to start with.'

'And the other?'

Chavasse shrugged. 'I'll leave that to fate.'

Yuan Tao nodded. 'Good, you are a wise man.' He frowned and then seemed to come to a decision. 'I can help you, but only if you place yourself completely in my hands. You must obey me in everything. Is that understood?'

'Perfectly. When do we start?'

'Tomorrow. You are prepared to stay here?'

'What about Su-yin?'

'She will not object. I am the head of the family since her father died. I told her I would stay two months. I think that should prove sufficient. If I am not mistaken, you have already studied *judo*?'

Chavasse shook his head. 'I concentrated on *karate*.'

'What grade?'

'Black belt, fifth *dan*.'

'This means nothing unless gained under the tutelage of a Japanese master.'

'It was. Yamakura.'

Yuan Tao's eyes widened with respect. 'A master indeed.' He smiled. 'I have a feeling we shall accomplish much, my dear Paul. But now we must eat. It is necessary to put flesh back upon your bones again.'

They left the bathroom and he led the way along a narrow corridor into the living-room at the far end. It was superbly furnished, a mixture of Chinese and European that was strangely attractive.

Su-yin was sitting by the fire and rose to greet them. She was wearing another *cheongsam* in green silk this time, embroidered with red poppies. Two discreet vents at each side of the skirt gave a glimpse of slender legs as she moved to meet them.

'I have news for you, my child,' Yuan Tao said. 'Mr. Chavasse will be staying with us for a while. I trust this will be convenient?'

'But of course, uncle.' She bowed her head slightly. 'And now I will bring the supper.'

She moved to the door, opened it and glanced back quickly over her shoulder at Chavasse and for the first time since he had known her, she was smiling.

CHAPTER THREE

In Motion, be Like Water ...

CHAVASSE CAME AWAKE EASILY FROM A deep dreamless sleep, aware at once of pale evening sunlight filtering in through the curtained window. He was alone and he turned to touch the pillow beside him for a moment before throwing back the single sheet which covered him. He padded across to the window and looked out through half-drawn curtains to the green vista of Hyde Park on the other side of Knightsbridge.

It was a beautiful evening, a slight breeze stirring the branches of the trees, sunlight glinting on the waters of the Serpentine in the distance and he turned and moved across to the wardrobe feeling calm and relaxed, alive and whole again.

His eyes sparkled, his head was clear and the slight ache in the pit of his stomach had one cause only—honest hunger. He stood in front of the dressing-table mirror and examined himself in the same slightly incredulous manner that had become something of a habit with him during the past three months. He looked younger, fitter in every way. The angry weal of the knife scar had faded into a thin white line and there was flesh on his bones again.

He could hear the sound of running water from the bathroom and when he opened the door, Su-yin was standing in the glass shower stall, her face turned up in ecstasy, hot water cascading over her shoulders and breasts, steam curling from the warm flesh.

She turned with a gay smile, gasping for breath. 'So you're awake at last.'

'No thanks to you. Why didn't you give me a shake?'

'You looked so peaceful, just like a baby.'

He grinned. 'Want me to scrub your back?'

'Not likely, you've caught me that way before and I'm supposed to be at the restaurant by nine o'clock.'

'But I thought we were having dinner together?'

She shook her head. 'Not tonight, Paul. Don't forget I have a business to run.' She smiled and dismissed him with a wave of one graceful hand. 'I shan't be long. Go and do one of your exercises or something.'

He closed the door and went back into his bedroom. It was cool and rather pleasant with the faint evening sunlight falling across the Indian carpet, bringing the colours vividly to life and the traffic outside sounded muted and unreal as if it was coming from another world.

He could almost hear the silence and stood there for a moment, relaxing completely, remembering the lines of the ancient Taoist verse that Yuan Tao had constantly repeated to him.

'In motion, be like water
At rest, like a mirror
Respond, like the echo
Be subtle as though non-existent.'

The ability to relax completely—this was the most important gift of all, a faculty retained by all other animals except Man. And cultivated, it could be the well-spring of a power that at times could be positively superhuman, for out of the quiet places, created by rigorous discipline and a system of training more than a thousand years old, sprang that intrinsic energy which the Chinese had named *ch'i*. The life force which in repose gave a man the pliability of a child and in action the explosive power of a tiger.

He sat down on the floor, relaxing completely, breathing in through his nose and out through his mouth slowly. He closed his eyes and covered his right ear with his left hand. He varied this after five minutes by covering his left ear with his right hand and after a further five minutes, covered both ears, arms crossed.

The darkness enfolded him like velvet and when he finally opened his eyes and straightened, his mouth was sharply cool, the tongue rigid. He took a long shuddering breath and stared into the shaft of sunlight from the window without blinking. When he got to his feet and walked to the wardrobe, his limbs seemed to be filled with power.

If he had gone to Mallory or anyone else and had spoken of this three months ago after his first meeting with Yuan Tao, they would have smiled pityingly. And yet the result was visible for all to see. A hand that no longer trembled, a clear eye and the kind of strength he would never have believed possible.

He took out an old tracksuit and as he pulled it on, Su-yin came in from the bathroom. She wore slacks and a Spanish shirt in vivid orange tied at the waist. Her dark hair swung loosely to her shoulders, framing the calm, beautiful face.

'You look pleased with yourself,' she said. 'Any special reason?'

He grinned. 'I've spent the afternoon in bed with a supremely beautiful woman and I still feel like Samson. That's reason enough.'

She started to laugh helplessly. 'Oh, Paul, you're quite hopeless. Ring for a taxi, will you? I'm going to be late.'

He phoned the porter quickly, replaced the receiver and moved towards her. 'You're not going until you agree to have dinner with me later. They can't need you all night. We could eat late and catch the midnight show at Twenty-one.'

He pulled her close and she sighed. 'It's quite impossible, I assure you.'

'Then I shan't let you go.'

He swung her up into his arms and carried her across to the bed. There was a brief struggle, punctuated by laughter and then his mouth found hers and they kissed.

She drew away with a sigh and looked up at him as he leaned over her. 'You're so different, so very different. Are you happy, Paul?'

'In spades. Thanks to Yuan Tao and you.'

'You have missed him since he returned to Hong Kong?'

'A great deal.'

'And would you miss me as much?'

He stopped smiling and sat up at once, frowning slightly. 'What is it? What's happened?'

'I'm going home, Paul,' she said simply.

'To Hong Kong?'

'That's right. I had a letter from my uncle this morning. My sister and her husband are opening a night club on Repulse Bay. They need me to help things get started.'

'What about the Red Dragon?'

She shrugged. 'It can continue quite adequately under management. I came to England for the experience, Paul, nothing more.'

'And what about me?'

'What are you trying to say? That you are in love with me?'

Chavasse hesitated, staring down at her and she shook her head. 'No, Paul, we've had a lot of fun together, but now it's time for me to go home.'

He took one of her hands and held it tight. 'It's going to take a little getting used to.'

She stood up. 'It'll take me two or three weeks to arrange things. This isn't the end.'

But she was wrong, they were both conscious of that as they went down in the lift and from now on, every meeting, every kiss would be coloured by the fact of her going.

They passed the porter at his desk and moved out through the swing doors. The taxi was waiting at the kerbside and Su-yin paused on top of the steps, a hand on his sleeve.

'No need to come down, Paul.' She kissed him briefly. 'You'll call me?'

'Of course.'

But he wouldn't, not again. He knew that suddenly and she knew it too, he could tell by the way she paused before getting into the taxi, turning to look up at him as if she was aware that it was for the last time, one hand raised in a brief little gesture that carried its own finality.

He was in the shower when the door-bell rang. He grabbed a towel, wrapped it around his waist and padded across to the front door, leaving damp footprints on the parquet floor.

When he opened the door a maid stood there wearing a blue nylon overall that was obligatory for all female staff. She was young and rather pretty with dark brown hair and hazel eyes.

'Mr. Chavasse, sir?' she said enquiringly, 'I've come to change the bed linen.'

'It's a hell of a funny time for that, isn't it?' Chavasse said.

'It should have been taken care of this afternoon, sir, but I believe you left word that you weren't to be disturbed.'

He grinned suddenly. 'I was forgetting. You're new, aren't you?'

She moved past him into the flat and nodded. 'That's right, sir.'

Chavasse closed the door. 'And what might your name be?'

'Peggy, sir.'

She had a faint Irish accent and smiled, colour staining her cheeks. Chavasse was suddenly aware of his nakedness and grinned. 'Sony, but you caught me in the shower. I'll leave you to it.'

He returned to the bathroom and stepped back into the shower. His stomach was aching for food and he faced the rest of the evening with pleasant anticipation, wondering where to eat, going over the possible choices one after the other in his mind.

He turned off the shower, stepped out of the stall and was at once aware of a strange sound in the living-room. He paused, frowning, then wrapped a towel about his waist and went through quickly.

Peggy was in the act of closing the front door and in the centre of the room stood a large laundry basket on rubber wheels. She turned and catching sight of Chavasse, smiled.

'Oh, there you are, sir.'

Chavasse nodded at the basket. 'What on earth's that thing doing in here?'

'The basket, sir?' She smiled and put a hand on it. 'Oh, the basket's for you, sir.'

The man who stepped in from the bedroom was of medium height and at least fifty with a kindly, wrinkled face. He wore white overalls and carried a Webley with a silencer fitted to the end of the barrel.

'Just lie down on the couch, hands behind your head, sir,' he said briskly.

'For God's sake,' Chavasse said. 'What is this?'

Peggy produced a flat black case from one pocket of her overalls. She opened it, took out a hypodermic and primed it briskly.

'Much better to do as he says, Mr. Chavasse.'

Chavasse took another look at the Webley and lay down on the couch. She came close, bending over him so close that for a moment he was aware of her perfume and then she pulled the towel away with a quick gesture and he felt the needle enter his right buttock.

Whatever it was, it was good, he had to give them that. It had roughly the effect of a rather soft blow from a hammer and he dived into dark waters.

He drifted up from a well of darkness and something exploded inside his head as a hand slapped him across the face. He felt no pain, that was the extraordinary thing. It was as if his body no longer belonged to him. Each sound seemed to come from somewhere in the middle distance and yet he could hear everything with the most astonishing clarity.

He opened his eyes slowly. The room was festooned with giant grey cobwebs that stretched from one wall to the other, and undulated slowly. He closed his eyes, breathing deeply, fighting back the panic that rose inside him. When he opened them again, the cobwebs had almost disappeared.

He was lying on a single bed against one wall of a large, square room. A shaded light hung down from the ceiling and curtains were drawn across the window. The only other furniture was a small table and a single chair which stood in the centre of the room.

Peggy, the Irish girl, was deep in conversation with a large man in an ill-fitting blue suit whose snow-white hair was close-cropped to the skull. They were speaking in Russian, and the girl's accent, while not wholly perfect to the trained ear, was still extremely good. The man was obviously Russian born, Georgian from the sound of him. Another man stood at the open door. He was of medium height, but heavily built with fair hair and an impassive face. He wore a neat white jacket of the type affected by medical orderlies in hospitals.

'You're sure he's all right?' the man in the blue suit said. 'Eight hours is a long time.'

'There's nothing to worry about,' the girl said. 'The dose was an exact one. There are individual variations in response, that's all. He could be out for another hour or two.'

'He must receive further sedation for the flight. We don't want any trouble.'

She nodded. 'It'll be taken care of. When will the plane leave?'

'I'm not sure. This damned fog might make things difficult and the pilot can't leave the airport without an official clearance. Whatever happens, his touchdown here can't last for longer than five minutes. We should be ready to go at any time during the next three hours.'

'I'll see to it,' she said.

He went out and she turned and walked across to the bed, immediately aware of Chavasse's fixed stare. She looked down at him calmly. 'So you're awake at last, are you? How do you feel?'

He moistened dry lips and managed a smile. 'Terrible.'

'A little coffee will soon fix that.' She spoke to the man at the door. 'See to it, Karl.'

He went out and the girl sat on the edge of the table and crossed one slim leg over the other. She was wearing a hip-length suede jacket and a neat skirt in Donegal tweed and, in any other circumstances, would have struck him as being extremely attractive.

Chavasse pushed himself up, discovering in the same moment that he was wearing his old tracksuit. Peggy immediately produced a Walther .32 from her pocket and held it in her lap. 'Just relax, Mr. Chavasse.'

'You know, you're good,' Chavasse said. 'Very good. A Dublin accent, suspiciously good Russian and legs to thank God for.'

She grinned. 'Flattery will get you nowhere.'

'One thing does puzzle me. What's a County Cork girl doing mixed up in a thing like this?'

'Wexford,' she said. 'And if you're interested, my father served ten years in an English prison for daring to fight for what he believed in.'

'Oh, no,' Chavasse groaned. 'Not that again.'

At that moment, an unearthly scream sounded from some lower floor and someone started to kick a door repeatedly.

He smiled brightly. 'What *is* this, a zoo?'

'It depends on your point of view,' she said. 'Most people come here for a rest cure.'

'Who for, their relatives?'

'Something like that. You could scream the place down and nobody would take the slightest notice.'

'Isn't that nice? This plane we're waiting for? Where's it taking me?'

'To visit some old friends of yours. They seem to think you may be able to help them in your retirement.'

'So from your point of view this is a strictly commercial proposition?'

'Exactly.' She got to her feet as Karl came back into the room with a tray. 'I must say I'm glad I was paid in advance. You don't strike me as being much of a bargain, Mr. Chavasse.'

Karl moved back to the door and she poured coffee into a blue mug. 'Would you like cream?'

'No, better make it black.'

She handed the mug to him and turned to Karl. 'You can take the tray away.'

In that single brief moment in which neither of them was looking at him, Chavasse poured his coffee into the space between the edge of the bed and the wall. When the girl turned to face him again, he was holding the empty mug to his mouth.

There was a sudden glint of amusement in her eyes that told him he had been right to be cautious. He pretended to drain the mug and leaned back, shaking his head from side to side as if suddenly drowsy.

As he closed his eyes, she chuckled. 'That's right, Mr. Chavasse. Just drift with the tide.'

Chavasse pushed himself up, allowing the mug to roll off the bed on to the floor, then fell back, head lolling to one side. He was aware of her cautious approach to the bed and schooled himself to take the sudden heavy slap across the face without flinching.

A step sounded in the doorway and the Russian spoke, sounding a little out of breath as if he had climbed the stairs too quickly. 'Karl told me he was awake.'

'Not any more,' Peggy said. 'He's just had a cup of black coffee laced with chloral hydrate. He'll be out for hours.'

'You're sure he'll be all right? He's of no use to us dead, you know.'

'You worry too much. Personally, I feel like an early breakfast. It's been a long night.'

They moved to the door. It closed and Chavasse heard two bolts rammed home and then a key turned in the lock. He swung his legs to the floor, sat there for a moment and then got to his feet.

The strange thing was that he felt no ill-effects at all except for a fierce hunger that gnawed at his empty belly as he moved to the door and listened. The voices faded away as though the two of them were descending a flight of stairs and then there was silence.

There was little point in wasting time on the door and he moved across to the window and pulled back the curtains. It was of the old-fashioned sash type and heavily barred. Rain drummed against the dirty glass and fifty or sixty feet below, a stone courtyard and outbuildings gleamed palely through the grey dawn. Beyond, rolling parkland was shrouded in a heavy, clinging mist.

He turned away and from somewhere in the depths of the building, a patient cried aloud, drumming on the door of his room and the sound was taken up by another and yet another, ugly and menacing.

The door was out and so was the window which left the floor or the roof. One thing was certain. Whatever he did had to be done quickly. He would certainly get no second chance.

He moved back to the window, crouched down and looked up and could just see a heavy iron gutter which at least proved that the false roof of the house was directly above the room or perhaps an attic. There was only one way of finding out. He dragged the table into the corner by the window, placed the chair on top of it and climbed up carefully.

The plaster of the ceiling was old and covered with a network of fine lines, so soft that when he raised his elbow into it sharply, a large piece fell away, a waterfall of white dust cascading after it. The noise being made by the inmates in the other part of the house was even louder now and Chavasse clawed at the edges of the hole, enlarging it quickly, tearing the wooden lathing away in great pieces. His fist went through and he could see into the false roof, light gleaming between chinks in the slates.

A couple of minutes later he was pulling himself up between two beams to crouch in the half darkness, covered in white dust. The false roof was extensive and obviously covered the whole house, a rabbit warren of strangely shaped eaves and half walls. He moved forward cautiously, walking on the beams and came to a trapdoor which had obviously been designed to give a more conventional access. He opened it carefully and looked down on to a tiny landing and below it, a narrow staircase, obviously leading from servants' quarters or something very much like them.

He dropped down and paused to listen. There was still a considerable disturbance going on elsewhere in the building, but fainter somehow and he started down the stairs quickly, stepping lightly on bare feet.

He paused on the next landing, peering over the rail for a moment before starting down and then a door on his left opened and Karl walked out, his mouth gaping in a wide yawn. In the same moment, he saw Chavasse and his eyes widened in alarm. Chavasse moved in fast, slamming his right fist into the man's stomach, lifting his knee into Karl's unprotected face as he keeled over, sending him backwards into the small room to sprawl across the bed.

He followed him in quickly, closing the door. Karl slid from the bed and rolled on the floor, moaning softly. Chavasse could find no gun on him and a quick search of the dressing-table drawers proved equally unsuccessful. He helped himself to a pair of rubber tennis shoes that were half a size too large for him, laced them up quickly and left.

At the bottom of the stairs he came to a narrow stone-flagged passage. A stale smell of cooking rose to meet him and somewhere to the left he could hear voices and the clatter of pans. He moved to the door at the end of the passage, opened it cautiously and looked out into the courtyard. It was quite deserted in the heavy rain except for an old green jeep parked a few yards away. He climbed inside quickly, pulled out the choke and pressed the starter. The engine turned over at once and a moment later, he was driving away.

Beyond the cobbled yard and the outhouses, a bridge took the road over a small stream, joining what was obviously the main drive very quickly. It was flanked by poplar trees, woodland fading into the grey morning on either side and he drove on, his eyes straining into the mist anxiously. There was a narrow turning to the left that disappeared into the trees and then he rounded a corner and braked suddenly.

Some twenty yards in front of him, the way was barred by iron gates, a steel mesh fence running into the mist on either side of it. The man who lounged beside the sentry box wore a peaked cap and semi-military uniform in dark blue, a black oilskin coat draped over his shoulders. He looked up quickly, flicking his cigarette away as the jeep braked to a halt. Chavasse hesitated, debating his chances of ramming the gate and then the man took an automatic rifle out of the sentry box and cocked it quickly.

As he raised it to his shoulders, Chavasse reversed round the corner quickly and from the direction of the house, the strange, unearthly wailing of a siren echoed through the morning in a dying fall.

He turned into the side track that he had noticed earlier and drove through trees as quickly as he dared, wheels bumping over the deep ruts and then the track simply petered out into a footpath, the undergrowth closing in on either side. He switched off the engine, jumped out and plunged into the trees running in the general direction of the fence.

He was soaked to the skin before he had gone twenty yards but didn't slacken his headlong course, one arm raised before him to protect his face from the flailing branches. He came out of the trees and paused on the edge of a strip of open parkland, the fence no more than ten yards away.

It was perhaps fifteen feet in height and angled over sharply at the top, but presented no particular problem to any reasonably active man, which was strange—and stranger still was the absence of even a single strand of barbed wire along the upper edge.

He picked up a large branch, moved forward and touched the fence gingerly. There was an immediate flash, a puff of blue smoke and the end of the branch burst into flame. He dropped it with a curse and somewhere behind him the hollow baying of a dog sounded on the morning air.

At least the heavy rain would kill his scent which solved one problem and he turned back into the wood and moved rapidly through the trees in the direction of the house. In the distance he could hear voices and the sound of a car on the main drive, but the siren had stopped.

He emerged on to a narrow path and ran along it quickly, swerving suddenly as the outbuildings at the back of the house loomed out of the mist. He crossed the small stream on foot, wading knee-deep, scrambled up the bank on the far side and peered round the corner of an old stable into the courtyard. There was no sign of life and he hurried across, opened the back door and went inside.

As he went back up the stairs he could still hear voices from the kitchen and the clatter of pans as someone prepared breakfast. Karl's door was closed. He stood listening outside for a moment, then turned the knob carefully and moved inside in one smooth movement.

Karl lay on the bed and Peggy leaned over him wiping blood from his face with a damp flannel. She turned with a frown and in the same moment threw the flannel at him, her hand diving into the pocket of her suede jacket.

Chavasse was too quick for her. As her hand came out, he grabbed for the wrist, twisting it so cruelly that she screamed with pain, dropping the Walther to the floor. He picked it up and backed away and she stood there, nursing her wrist, strangely calm.

'You didn't get very far, did you?'

'Unfortunately not,' Chavasse said. 'The man on the gate had an automatic rifle and the fence was hot enough to fry eggs on. There are other ways, however.'

'Such as?'

He pulled her close, his fingers hooking into her arm so that she winced. 'You and I are going to take a little walk. I'd like you to introduce me to that friend of yours, the agitated gentleman who's supposed to be in charge round here. I'm sure we can come to some arrangement.'

She opened her mouth as if to protest and then seemed to change her mind. 'It won't get you very far.'

'I wouldn't be too sure about that,' Chavasse told her and he held open the door with a slight, mocking bow.

She led the way up the stairs to the next landing and turned along a narrow corridor which finally emerged on to a great circular landing beneath a domed roof, what was obviously the entrance hall of the house below them.

He peered over cautiously as someone crossed the black and white tiled floor below and disappeared. 'Where to now?' he whispered.

'The next landing,' she said and they started down the curving Regency staircase.

It was so quiet that he could hear the ticking of a grandfather clock standing in a corner and when they paused outside the door she indicated, he could hear nothing.

'Open it,' he said. 'Very, very quietly and remember I'm right behind you.'

The door swung in smoothly without a sound and he gave her a slight push forward. The walls of the room were lined with books, logs burning brightly in an Adam fireplace to the left.

The man who stood at the open window listening to the sounds of the chase in the park beyond, seemed strangely familiar. For a moment, Chavasse thought he was going mad and then a door clicked open on his right.

An amused, familiar voice said, 'Good morning, Paul,' and he swung to find Jean Frazer standing there, a tray in her hands.

Chavasse glanced back at the window and Graham Mallory turned and smiled. 'Ah, there you are, Paul. Well, this is famous. You really must allow me to congratulate you.'

CHAPTER FOUR

THE MAN FROM RUM JUNGLE

WHEN CHAVASSE TURNED, PEGGY HAD WITHDRAWN, closing the door behind her. Jean Frazer put down the tray on a small coffee table beside the fire.

'Better have a cup of tea, Paul,' she said calmly. 'You look as if you could do with one.'

Chavasse tossed the Walther on to the desk. 'Are you trying to tell me this whole thing was a put-up job?' he said to Mallory.

'A test, Paul. A practical test which I decided might save me a great deal of time and indicate just how true the reports I've been getting on you were. I must say you're looking remarkably fit.'

'And the girl?' Chavasse said. 'Peggy or whatever she calls herself. She's one of your people?'

'Margaret Ryan,' Mallory said. 'Nice girl. Not been with us long. A trainee on the special course. They all are here. A new place we opened a couple of months back. I think everyone put up a rather convincing show, don't you?'

'So did I, I'm afraid I've made rather a mess of one of your boys.'

'All in the game. Mind you, Peggy was beginning to have her doubts about the great Paul Chavasse, especially when you appeared to drink the coffee.'

'She missed out on that,' Chavasse said. 'And another thing. Her Russian wouldn't stand up for five minutes anywhere east of Berlin, not with that Dublin accent of hers.'

'Oh, I don't know,' Mallory said. 'She's an Irish citizen which can be rather useful. They don't even need a visa for Red China. An unusual virtue in this day and age.'

Chavasse stood in front of the fire, steam curling from the wet tracksuit and accepted the tea Jean handed to him gratefully.

'I'll run you a bath, Paul,' she said and went through into the bedroom.

'Yes, I really must congratulate you,' Mallory went on. 'You're quite your old self again, only more so. What would you like for breakfast?'

'Two of everything,' Chavasse said. 'And lots of strong black coffee, Turkish for preference. And would you mind telling me what this is all about?'

'Later, Paul,' Mallory said. 'You'll find some of your own clothes in the bedroom. I thought you might be needing them. Don't be long. We've got a lot to discuss.'

'I bet we have,' Chavasse said sourly, but as he went through into the bedroom, he was smiling and excitement moved inside him like a cold sword.

His favourite grey flannel suit was neatly laid out on the bed together with shirt and underclothes. As he paused to examine them, Jean Frazer came out of the bathroom.

'You think of everything, don't you?' he said.

She smiled and there was a touch of colour in her cheeks. 'It's good to have you back, Paul.'

She started to move away and he caught her hand. 'What's it all about, Jean? Something big?'

She nodded slowly, her face serious. 'Better let him tell you, Paul. You know what he's like.'

The door closed behind her and he stood staring into space, wondering what it was that Mallory had in store for him. But what the hell. Life began again. He went into the bathroom and stripped off the tracksuit.

'It really is remarkable,' Mallory said as Chavasse poured his third cup of coffee. 'If I hadn't seen it with my own eyes I don't think I could have believed it. This chap Yuan Tao must be quite something.'

Chavasse paused, the cup half way to his mouth. 'So you know about him?'

'Naturally.'

'You must have had me watched pretty closely. Now that's something I can't understand. I thought you'd written me off?'

'Let's just say I didn't like to see you go and then I started getting daily reports which were more than interesting. Your friend could make a fortune if he set himself up in business.'

'He wouldn't be interested,' Chavasse said. 'He has one already, together with three factories in Hong Kong and a half interest in one of the biggest shipping lines in the Far East.'

'Yes, I was aware of that.'

'I thought you might be.'

'His niece seems a very attractive girl.'

'She's returning to Hong Kong next week,' Chavasse said. 'I bet that's something you *didn't* know.'

'What a pity. We'll just have to find something else to fill your time.'

'I'm sure you won't have the slightest difficulty.' Chavasse lit a cigarette and blew out a cloud of smoke with a sigh of satisfaction. 'What's it all about?'

'To tell you the truth, I'm not sure.' Mallory went to the desk, unlocked a drawer and took out a buff file. 'Have you ever heard of a man called Max Donner?'

'The financier?' Chavasse nodded. 'You see him in the society columns all the time. Australian, isn't he?'

'That's right. Comes from a place called Rum Jungle, south of Darwin in the Northern Territory. There's a hell of a lot of development going on there now, but in Donner's day it was just a dot on the map.' Mallory opened the file and pushed it across. 'Have a look at the photos.'

Donner was a magnificent figure of a man, at least six feet three in height with a great breadth of shoulder, and dark hair swept back over his ears. The photos showed him in every possible aspect. Mingling with the stars at a film premiere, playing polo, shooting grouse, even shaking hands with Royalty at a Variety Club charity dinner and he was always smiling.

'How old is he?'

'Fifty.'

Chavasse was surprised. 'He doesn't look anywhere near that. He seems to live a full life.'

'He can afford to. At the last count he was worth at least a million and moving up fast. Not bad for an ex-Australian infantry sergeant with no formal education.'

The last photo showed Donner on his yacht in Cannes harbour, reclining in a deck chair, glass in hand, gazing up at the young girl who leaned against the rail beside him. She was perhaps sixteen and wore a bikini, long blonde hair to her shoulders, blowing in the breeze, half-obscuring her face.

'Who's this?' Chavasse said, holding up the photo.

'His step-daughter, Asta Svensson.'

'Swedish?'

'Right through to her pretty backbone. That was taken three years ago. She's nineteen now and very, very attractive.'

'I think Donner would agree with you to judge from the way he's looking at her on this picture.'

'What makes you say that?'

'He's smiling on all the others, but not on this one. It's as if he's saying, "You, I take seriously." Where does her mother fit in?'

'She died about three months before that picture was taken. She was drowned skin-diving off some Greek island or other, but you can read through the file later. I'll just give you an outline for the moment. It'll save time.'

He got to his feet, moved to the fire and started to fill his pipe. 'Max Donner is typical of a certain type of man who's rocketed to the top in this country since the war. Mostly they started with nothing and the boom in property and land values helped them along.'

'When did he arrive?'

'1948. Company Sergeant Major in an Australian infantry battalion when he was demobbed in '47. Good solid war record in the Western Desert, and New Guinea. He picked up the Military Medal there, by the way.'

'And how did he set about making a million from scratch in a strange land? I'd love to know.'

'Simple really, or at least he makes it look that way. The *Sunday Times* did a feature on him the other year. "The Man from Rum Jungle," they called it. There's a copy in the file. First of all he took a job as a salesman. Reconditioned car engines, then textile machinery. Fifteen hundred a year and a company car—good money for the hungry forties. Most men would have been satisfied.'

'But not Donner?'

'Not Donner. He went into partnership with a man called Victor Wiseman. They bought an old Victorian house in Kensington in January, 1950, for three thousand pounds with the aid of a substantial mortgage and converted it into four flats which they sold separately over the next six months for a total of seven thousand, three hundred.'

Chavasse pursed his lips in a soundless whistle. 'And never looked back.'

'Donner certainly didn't. Wiseman dropped out with his half when they reached twenty thousand and bought himself a restaurant in Clapham. You've got to take chances in the property game and he just didn't have the stomach for it.'

'He must have been kicking himself ever since.'

'I expect so. Our friend was doing so well by 1952 that he was able to form the Donner Development Corporation. One of the first outfits to get in on multi-storey office block building in the city centres. Later, he formed his own finance company. Hire purchase for the millions. The biggest golden goose of all.'

'I should have thought he would have been worth rather more than your million by now?'

'You should see what he spends. He believes in living life to the full and he's made some enormous donations to some of the new universities.'

'When did he get married?'

'1955. To Gunilla Svensson, widow of a Swedish stockbroker who'd handled Donner's affairs in Stockholm.'

'A love match?'

Mallory shrugged. 'It certainly looked that way at the time, especially if you go by what the gossip columnists were saying. I should think it quite possible. She was a very beautiful woman.'

'And what about the daughter. Presumably Donner's her guardian?'

'That's right. She has relatives in the States, but none in Sweden or this country. She was at Heathfield till she was seventeen then did a year at finishing school in Paris. She's spent this last year at Stockholm University studying Sociology.'

'Doesn't she ever come home?'

'She's stayed with him frequently in London if that's what you mean and he usually flies across to see her once a month.'

Chavasse nodded. 'Takes his parental responsibilities seriously then?'

'It certainly looks that way. From all accounts there can be little doubt about the genuineness of his affection for her.'

'And what about her?'

'One can't be certain. On the other hand she doesn't have a great deal of choice in the matter. Her mother left her a sizeable fortune, but Donner holds it on trust for her until she's twenty-five.'

'An interesting situation,' Chavasse said. 'But where does it all lead?'

'I'm not really sure. That's where you come in. About six months ago, M.I.6. handled a very minor espionage affair. You may remember it. An Admiralty clerk called Simmons was caught passing classified information to a man called Ranevsky, a naval attaché at the Russian Embassy.'

'He got five years, didn't he?'

'That's right. It was all very small beer.'

'Didn't the Russian claim diplomatic immunity?'

Mallory nodded. 'M.I.6. had him for a couple of hours and then he had to be handed over to his own people. They flew him out next morning. The really interesting thing proved to be the fifty one-pound notes he'd passed over to Simmons before they were arrested. They were new notes and M.I.6. managed to trace them to a Bond Street bank where a cashier not only recognised Ranevsky's photograph, but also remembered details of the cheque he'd cashed.'

'Are you saying it was one of Donner's?'

Mallory nodded. 'Genuine, too.'

'What did Donner have to say?'

'He wasn't asked anything, Paul. That side of things was never mentioned at Simmons's trial. It wasn't worth wasting on such an insignificant event. They simply dropped the whole thing fairly and squarely into my lap and told me to get on with it.'

'And you've been checking on Donner ever since?'

'That's right and the deeper we probe, the unhealthier it looks. From Burgess and Maclean onwards, everywhere we dig, we seem to find Max Donner hovering on the outer perimeter of things. And not only here. France, Germany, Canada—he has business interests all over the place.'

'But Donner's a highly successful business man, a respected public figure?' Chavasse shook his head. 'What would he stand to gain? It just doesn't make sense.'

'Neither did the Gordon Lonsdale affair at first.'

'But Lonsdale was a Russian, a professional agent.'

'Who was a Canadian to all intents and purposes. Even now there is some doubt about his real name.'

'Are you suggesting that Max Donner might be another Lonsdale?'

'I'm not sure,' Mallory said. 'It's a possibility: that's all we can say for certain at the moment. Donner's parents were Austrian. He was born in Vienna in 1916 while his father was fighting on the Italian front. After the war, things were difficult and then his father came into a small legacy and they emigrated to Australia in 1925.'

'How did they fetch up in a place like Rum Jungle?'

'Like plenty before him, Donner's father fell into the wrong hands. With what was left of his legacy he bought what he understood to be a thriving cattle station. When they got there, they found a mud hole in the wilderness, a broken down shack and a handful of starving cows. Mrs. Donner wasn't built for that kind of life. She died in 1930.'

'When the boy was fourteen?'

'That's right. He and his father hung on for another year, then sold out for seventy-five pounds and left.'

'Where for—Sydney?'

'With a depression just beginning?' Mallory shook his head. 'They took to the road in the Outback following that great Australian custom like thousands of others. Donner's father died in 1933 at a place called Clay Crossing. We know that from the death certificate.'

'When the boy was seventeen?'

Mallory nodded. 'From then on, he was on his own. Just another swagman walking the Outback at a time when half the men in the country were out of work. He joined the army in Kalgoorlie the day after war was declared.'

'And you don't know what happened in between?'

Mallory shook his head. 'From the death of his father at Clay Crossing in 1933 to his enlistment in the army in 1939—a great big blank and I don't like it.'

'And what's he up to at this end?'

'I'm not sure, that's the trouble, but I could make a reasonable guess. For the past couple of years, we've been losing people in a steady trickle. People like Simmons. Not all that important, but important enough. Confidential clerks engaged on classified work, cypher clerks and so on. Thirty-eight in all.'

'Too many,' Chavasse said. 'Only a really efficient organisation could tackle such a number.'

'And an organisation that never misses. This is really classified information, Paul, but twice during the same period, we've been about to arrest a really big fish. In each case he's been spirited away.'

'Forty in all,' Chavasse said. 'That's really very good.'

'Add to those, eleven poor devils who having defected to this country and having applied for and been granted, political asylum, have also completely disappeared. And they've turned up again on the other side, by the way.'

'You're sure about that?'

'Certain. As a matter of fact we've just lost another this week. A rocket expert called Boris Souvorin. Even our American friends didn't know we had him.'

'And you think Donner's behind all this?'

'I'm certain of it. He's been hovering on the fringe in too many cases for my peace of mind.'

'Couldn't you pull him in?'

'On what charge?'

'What about that bearer cheque of his that Ranevsky cashed? Wouldn't that do for a start?'

'Not a chance.' Mallory shook his head. 'Everything would depend upon the bank clerk's evidence that the cheque Ranevsky cashed *was* Donner's. He wouldn't last ten minutes on the witness stand with a really good counsel having a go at him. Everything else is merely supposition and guesswork.'

'Which you happen to believe?'

'I've never been more certain of anything in my life.'

'Then what are you doing about it?'

Mallory applied another match to the bowl of his pipe. 'How well do you know North-West Scotland and the Hebrides?'

'I went for a climbing holiday in Skye when I was seventeen. I don't think I've ever been back. Why—is it important?'

'There's a place called Moidart on the north-west coast between Loch Shiel and the sea. About a hundred and twenty square miles of mountain and moorland, very sparsely inhabited. A wild, lonely place. Donner bought a house and ten thousand acres of deer forest up there about eighteen months ago.'

'Did he now,' Chavasse said. 'And why would a fun-loving boy like Max Donner suddenly take to the highlands like that? I thought Cap d'Antibes was his stamping ground.'

'So did I.'

'Is there anything in particular he could be after up there?'

'I don't think so.'

Mallory took a map of Scotland from a drawer in his desk and unrolled it. 'There's the atomic submarine base at Holy Loch, of course, and various missile testing ranges in the Outer Hebrides. At Lewis, for instance and South Uist and here at Fhada, south of Barra.'

'Any research work going on there?'

'Not within the meaning of the term, although there's some very interesting stuff being handled. We aren't quite the laggards in the rocket business that some people would like to imagine. No, the places I've mentioned are mainly used for personnel training and test firing. The training part is one of our NATO commitments and very important. Of course the French don't come any more, but we regularly train personnel from German army guided missile regiments.'

'I'd have thought there would be plenty there to interest Donner?'

Mallory shook his head. 'He wouldn't get within smelling distance of one of these places. Civilians aren't even allowed to land and as regards seeing the damned things go up ...' He shrugged. 'Plenty of foreign trawlers, Russian and otherwise, fish those waters.'

'Then what's he doing there?'

Mallory tapped a finger on the map. 'There's Moidart and there's Donner's estate, Glenmore, a bare half mile from the sea. As I've already said, a wild, lonely place with few people about. A trawler, or even a submarine, could run in close most nights without being observed.'

'So you think that's the other end of his pipeline?'

'Certain of it. He had a similar house on the Pembrokeshire coast in Wales for six years. He moved when a dam project started five miles away.'

Chavasse nodded. 'I must say it sounds likely. Is Donner in residence?'

'He flew up in his private plane the day before yesterday.'

'Do you think he took Souvorin with him?'

Mallory shrugged. 'He certainly wasn't visible. No, I don't think he'd take that kind of risk. If he is behind Souvorin's disappearance, he'll have shipped him north by some other route. I'm certain of that.'

'And if he is there, how do we prove it? If this place is as isolated as you say it is, I'd stick out like a sore thumb.'

'I've taken care of that,' Mallory said, 'and rather ingeniously, though I do say it myself. There's a small estate about ten miles from Donner's place, called Ardmurchan Lodge. A five-year lease was offered a month ago with three thousand acres of deer forest adjoining Donner's property so I snapped it up and dug a friend of mine out of retirement to play tenant, an old M.I.5 man, Colonel Duncan Craig. He's seventy if he's a day. Officially he'll be your uncle.'

'And what am I supposed to be doing there?'

'You'll be on vacation. Lecturer in French Literature at the University of Essex. I've fixed the whole thing up officially. As a matter of fact, they're expecting you to start in October.'

'Presumably Craig's been nosing around up there already?'

'Not really, although he has sent us some useful information. He's an old man, remember. Active for his age, but still an old man. I was hoping he might strike up an acquaintance with Donner, but it hasn't worked out. He's met him three or four times. Apparently, Donner's always perfectly civil, but hasn't handed out any invitations to Glenmore House.'

'Then how do I get in?'

Mallory held up the photo of Donner and his stepdaughter. 'There's always the girl.'

Chavasse frowned. 'How?'

'Wait and see.' Mallory pressed a buzzer on his desk.

A moment later, the door opened and Peggy Ryan entered. She moved to the desk, a slight, calm smile on her face. 'You wanted me, Mr. Mallory?'

'Yes, Peggy. Tell Mr. Chavasse about Asta Svensson.'

Peggy turned to face him. 'I was enrolled at the University of Stockholm at the beginning of last term, ostensibly as an exchange student.'

'The idea being to cultivate Asta Svensson's acquaintance?'

She nodded. 'She's a nice girl, Mr. Chavasse. We became great friends.'

'What about Donner? How does she get on with him?'

'I think she's a little afraid of him. He visited her twice while I was there. Nothing's too good for her as far as he's concerned. He's taking her on a tour of the Far East this vacation.'

'When do they leave?'

'He's joining Asta in Stockholm ten days from now. They're to fly from there.' She smiled. 'He's in for a surprise, though.'

'What do you mean?'

'This place of his in Scotland—Asta's never been. Apparently he's always fobbed her off with grimy old Nice or Cannes or somewhere instead.'

'So she's decided to take the law into her own hands?'

'If she hasn't changed her plans since I left her four days ago, she should be flying in to Glasgow tomorrow morning. She intends to carry on from there by train and arrive unannounced. Poor kid—I hope she makes out all right.'

'You liked her, didn't you?'

'A lot better than her step-father. He's the kind of man who smiles with his face only, never with his eyes.'

'And you don't think she's mixed up in his affairs?'

Peggy shook her head firmly. 'Not a chance.'

Chavasse nodded. 'All right, Peggy. Thanks.'

The Irish girl looked at Mallory who nodded. She moved to the door, opened it and turned with a smile. 'And Mr. Chavasse, I don't know just how susceptible you are, but I'd better warn you. I don't think you've ever seen anything in a skirt that could be an improvement on Asta Svensson.'

The door closed before he could reply. Mallory chuckled and took several more photos out of the folder. 'Better have a look at these, Paul. I think you'll see what she means.'

Chavasse only needed to look at the first one to see what three years had done to the child in the bikini. She gazed out at him calmly, lips slightly parted, the hair, so blonde that it was almost white, hanging to her shoulders. She was standing on a sand dune, the sea behind her, the strong sunlight outlining her firm young thighs perfectly through the thin cotton of the simple dress she wore. And those eyes. They seemed to look through and beyond him and his throat went dry. It was as if he had been waiting for this girl all his life.

CHAPTER FIVE

NIGHT ON A BARE MOUNTAIN

IT WAS VERY PEACEFUL IN THE small station by the lochside and Chavasse peered out of the window of the rear compartment keeping out of sight. On the other side of the glen, the mountain reared its bald head more than three thousand feet into a clear blue sky, sunlight glinting on a waterfall high on the slope that spilled in a white apron across granite to disappear into the birch trees that fringed the base.

A door opened in the front coach and Asta Svensson stepped down on to the platform. She wore a soft leather jacket, a pleated tweed skirt, nylon stockings and handmade leather brogues.

With the pale blonde hair glinting in the sunlight, she made an attractive, vibrant figure in the quiet setting of the little railway station. She moved across to the ticket collector who stood at the barrier beside the small waiting room. There was some conversation, a burst of laughter and she went out through the barrier.

Chavasse waited, wondering what she was up to. Following her from Glasgow to Fort William had been easy, for the train had been quite busy, but the branch line to Arisaig and Mallaig was little used now that the holiday season was over and he'd had difficulty keeping out of sight.

The ticket collector moved to join the guard as he emerged from the waiting room. 'You've lost a passenger, Tam,' he said in a soft highland *blas*.

'Is that a fact now?' the guard observed calmly.

'Aye, a bonny lass with hair of corn and a face to thank God for. A Miss Svennson. Her step-father's yon fella Donner that bought Glenmore last year. She's away over the mountain. You're to put down her baggage at Lochailort.'

'I hope it keeps fine for her.' The guard took out his watch. 'The long short cut she'll find it if the weather breaks.'

Chavasse reached for his raincoat, opened the door and got out. 'Did I hear you say there was a short cut over the mountain?'

'Well now, sir, and that would depend on where you want to be.'

'Ardmurchan Lodge.'

The guard nodded. 'Over the top of Ben Breac and a twelve mile walk on the other side. You'll be staying with Colonel Craig, the new tenant?'

'My uncle. He'll be waiting for me at Lochailort. Perhaps you'd be good enough to tell him where I am?'

The five shillings he slipped into the guard's hand was pocketed without inspection. 'Leave it to me, sir.'

He blew his whistle and boarded the train. As it moved away from the platform, Chavasse turned to the ticket collector. 'And where do I go from here?'

'Through the village and over the bridge, sir. You'll find a path through the birches on your left. It's hard going, but you can't miss the cairns that mark the way. Once over the top, the track is plain to the glen below.'

'Do you think the weather will hold?'

The ticket collector squinted up at the mountain. 'A touch of mist perhaps and rain in the evening. I shouldn't waste time on top.' He smiled suddenly. 'I'd tell the young lady that if I were you, sir. It's no place for a lassie to be on her own.'

Chavasse grinned. 'I'll do that. A pity to see her get wet.'

'A thousand pities, sir.'

At a small general store he purchased an extra packet of cigarettes and two half-pound bars of milk chocolate. Twelve miles on the other side of the mountain, the ticket collector had said and that wasn't counting the miles that stood up on end. A long walk and something told him he might be hungry before the end of it.

He marched down the quiet village street, his raincoat slung over one shoulder and crossed the bridge over a clear flowing stream. It was still and quiet in the hot afternoon sun and the road stretched before him, lifting upwards and away from the waters of the loch shining through the trees below.

There was no sign of the girl which suited him for the moment. Sooner or later a meeting was inevitable, in fact necessary, but he preferred that it should be at a time and place of his own choosing.

The track snaked up through the birch trees, lifting steeply, bracken pressing in on either side. It was cool and dark and somehow remote from the world, the path dappled with light where shafts of sunlight pierced the roof of green branches.

The trees grew sparser until he moved out on to a slope where the track disappeared into bracken that in places was waist high. Occasionally grouse or plover lifted out of the heather, disturbed by his passing. He moved up over a steep ridge and found himself on the edge of a boulder-strewn plain that lifted to meet the lower slopes of Ben Breac.

In the same moment he saw the girl, up on the shoulder of the mountain to his right, six or seven hundred feet above him.

She paused, turning to look out over the loch and he dropped back into cover. When he peered cautiously over the edge of the ridge a moment later, she had disappeared round the shoulder of the mountain.

She was certainly moving fast. Faster than he would have thought possible, but hardly surprising, remembering her litheness and the healthy glow of her golden skin and he took out an ordnance survey map of Moidart and unfolded it. The track she was following was plainly marked, skirting the shoulder of the mountain, climbing gradually to the final plateau and the summit. There was a quicker way, of course—straight up. But only a fool would try that.

Chavasse raised his eyes to the swelling breast of the mountain above, the great wall of granite beyond. A steady eye and strong nerves were all that was needed and he could be sitting on the summit cairn waiting to greet her when she arrived. He folded the map, put it away and started to climb.

It was easy enough on the lower slopes with the heather springy to the feet, but within half an hour, he came out onto a great cascading bank of scree and loose stones that moved alarmingly beneath him with each step he took, bringing the heart into his mouth.

He worked his way to the left, making for the waterfall he had observed from the train, and when he reached it, followed the channel upwards, jumping from one great boulder to the other. Finally, he moved out on to a small plateau and faced the granite cliffs.

From the station, they had looked impossible, but now he was close enough to see that instead of being perpendicular, they leaned backwards gently in a series of great tilted slabs, cracked and fissured by the years.

He paused for as long as it took him to eat half a bar of chocolate, then slung his raincoat over his back, fastening it securely with its own belt and started to climb.

He wondered how the girl was doing, but there was no means of knowing, for the shoulder of the mountain was between them, and he climbed on, testing each hold securely before moving. He turned once to look down into the glen and saw the ticket collector moving from the station to his small cottage adjoining. When he looked down again half an hour later, he could see nothing, and suddenly a cold wind seemed to move across his face.

He climbed on doggedly and as he scrambled over the edge of a great up-tilted slab of granite a few minutes later, grey mist spilled across the face of the mountain with incredible speed, wrapping itself around him like some living thing.

He had spent enough time in hill country in various parts of the world to have learned that in such circumstances it was fatal to make any kind of move at all unless there was a well defined track to follow. Remembering what lay beneath him, he sat down between a couple of boulders and lit a cigarette.

He had a long wait and it was just over an hour later when a sudden current of air snatched the grey curtain away and beyond, the valleys lay dark and quiet in the evening sunlight, the mountains touched with a golden glow.

He started to climb again and an hour later came over the final edge and found himself on a gently sloping plateau that lifted to meet the sky a quarter of a mile away, a great cairn of stones marking the ultimate peak.

There was no sign of Asta Svensson and when he cut across the track, he turned and hurried back along it until he reached a point where he had a clear view of its zigzag course for two thousand feet up the great northern slope of the mountain.

So she had beaten him to the summit—so much was obvious. But that was hardly surprising, for with the track to follow, the mist must have proved no problem at all. He turned and trudged along the track towards the cairn, feeling suddenly tired for the first time. Tired and annoyed. He'd tried to be clever and he'd made a mess of it, it was as simple as that. Far better to have struck up a conversation with her in the train while he'd had the chance.

He moved towards the cairn, head bowed as he took the final slope and then he paused, the breath hissing sharply between his teeth at the vision of splendour unfolded before him.

The sea was still in the calm evening, the islands so close that it was as if he had only to reach out to be able to touch the Rum and Eigg and Skye beyond, on the dark horizon, the final barrier against the Atlantic, the Outer Hebrides.

Below, a small loch cut deep into the heart of the hills, black with depth in the centre, purple and grey where granite edges lifted to the surface, and on Skye the peaks of the mountains were streaked with orange.

The beauty of it was too much for a man and with an inexplicable dryness in his throat, he turned and hurried along the track down into Glenmore.

Asta Svensson was tired and her right ankle was beginning to ache rather badly, legacy of an old skiing injury. It had taken her much longer to cross the mountain than she had imagined. Now she was faced with a twelve mile walk before reaching her destination, and what had originally seemed a rather amusing idea was fast turning into something of an ordeal.

The track which followed the lochside was dry and dusty and hard to the feet. After a while, she turned a bend and found her way barred by a five-barred gate, a wire fence running into the bracken on either side.

The notice said, *Keep Out—Glenmore Estate—Private,* and the gate was padlocked. She hoisted herself over, surprised at the effort it took, slipped and fell on the other side and a sudden stab of pain in her right ankle told her that she had turned it.

She got to her feet and started to walk again, limping heavily, and as she turned a curve in the glen she saw a small hunting lodge in a green loop of grass beside the loch. The door was locked, but when she went round to the rear, a window stood an inch or two ajar. She opened it without difficulty, pulled up her skirt and climbed over the sill.

When she struck a match she found herself standing in a small, well-fitted kitchen which, from the look of it, had been added to the main building only recently. There was a calor gas stove in one corner, an oil lamp on a bench beside it. She lit the lamp expertly, remembering with a strange nostalgia, holidays on her grandmother's farm on Lake Siljah as a little girl and went into the other room.

It was adequately furnished and quite comfortable in spite of the whitewashed walls and polished wood floor. A fire was laid on the stone hearth. She put a match to it, then sat in one of the wing-backed chairs and rested her right leg on a stool.

The dry wood flared up quickly. She added pine logs from the stack at the side of the hearth and suddenly she was warm again and her ankle seemed to have eased. She took off her leather jacket, hung it over the back of her chair and lit a cigarette, pausing at the alien sound in the distance.

Within a moment or two she knew what it was—a vehicle of some sort being driven surprisingly fast considering the conditions. She sat there waiting and then the noise of it seemed to fill the night and it braked to a halt outside. There was a quick step, the rattle of a key in the lock and the door was flung open.

The man who stood there was of medium height with a weak, sullen face and badly needed a shave. He wore a shabby tweed suit that was a size too large for him and yellow hair poked untidily from beneath the tweed cap.

He held a double-barrelled shotgun in both hands, and lowered it slowly, astonishment on his face. 'Would ye look at that now?'

Asta returned his gaze calmly. 'What do you want?'

'What do I want?' He laughed harshly. 'Now that's a good one. You're trespassing, did you know that? And how the hell did you get in here anyway?'

'Through the kitchen window.'

He shook his head and ran his tongue over his lips quickly, his eyes on her legs, on the skirt that was rucked up above her knees.

'I don't think my boss would like that at all. He's very particular about things like that. I mean, if he knew, he might even consider calling in the police.'

His eyes carried their own message and she took her foot off the stool and pulled down her skirt. 'I turned my ankle back there on the track somewhere. I've just come over Ben Breac.'

'Oh, a hiker? That's nice.'

Asta took a deep breath and stood up, not in the least afraid. 'It's lucky you came. You'll be able to give me a lift, won't you?'

He reached out, clutching at her arm. 'That depends now, doesn't it?'

She was tired and the blotched whisky face was suddenly completely repulsive. 'What's your name?'

He grinned. 'That's more friendly. It's Fergus—Fergus Munro.'

She pulled her arm free and sent him staggering with a vigorous shove of both hands.

'Then don't be stupid, Fergus Munro.'

For a moment he gaped in astonishment and then anger twisted his mouth. He dropped the shotgun and grabbed at her as she turned away, fingers hooking into the neck of her blouse, the thin material ripping along the seam of one shoulder.

She gave a cry of anger, striking out at him, aware of his hands on her, the staleness of his breath, the blotched, drink-sodden face and then beyond him, she saw a man materialise from the darkness to stand in the doorway.

It was the face which held her, the handsome, devil's face, eyes like black holes above high cheekbones, full of cold fury, flaring into a ruthless action that was almost frightening in its efficiency.

One hand fastened on her assailant's collar, another in his belt, tearing him away from her, sending him across the room with a tremendous heave.

Munro crashed against the opposite wall and slid to his knees. For a moment he stayed there, staring up at Chavasse, bewilderment on his face and then he flung himself forward, reaching for the shotgun.

Chavasse kicked it away from him, grabbed for the man's right wrist with both hands, twisting it round and up in an *akaido* shoulder lock, and sent him head first across the room to crash into the wall for the second time.

When Munro picked himself up, blood trickled down his cheek from a cut above the right eye and his face was contorted with fear. He plunged for the open door in complete panic and Chavasse went after him.

'Let him go!' Asta cried sharply.

Chavasse paused, a hand on each side of the door frame and when he turned, the killing mask was still firmly in place. And then he smiled, becoming in that moment almost a different person.

'Are you all right, Miss Svensson?'

She nodded slowly. 'Who are you?'

'My name is Chavasse—Paul Chavasse.'

Outside, the engine of Fergus Munro's Land Rover roared into life and he drove rapidly away down the glen. Chavasse closed the door and when he turned she was sitting in the wing-backed chair again, her right leg back on the footstool.

She chuckled suddenly. 'You know, I was really beginning to despair, Mr. Chavasse. I thought you were never going to catch up with me.'

CHAPTER SIX

CHOCOLATES
AND KISSES

'WAS I THAT OBVIOUS?' CHAVASSE SAID lightly.

'But of course. On the station platform at Glasgow, that French face of yours stuck out like a sore thumb.'

'Breton,' he said.'

'Is there a difference?'

'My grandfather has forcible opinions on that score.'

'I concede the point.'

'I kiss your hands on his behalf.'

'Oh, no you don't,' she said quickly. 'Or at least not until you've explained yourself. When you appeared again on the platform at Fort William waiting for the Mallaig train, I was intrigued to say the least. Something of a coincidence, considering there were only five passengers in all.'

'But life is full of coincidences,' Chavasse said. 'One of the many things which make it so interesting.'

'Was it a coincidence that you followed me over the mountain?'

'Did I?'

'I saw you when I stopped for my first breather and looked back.'

'Presumably I was a little too late in dropping out of sight—'

'You were.'

A slow smile spread across his face. 'You didn't by any remote chance leave the train deliberately, just to draw me on.'

'But of course,' she said calmly. 'What else could a poor girl do? I was beginning to despair of you and then I consulted my map and saw that there was a way over the mountain to where I wanted to be.' She smiled enchantingly. 'And it was such a beautiful afternoon. A pity to be cooped up in a stuffy carriage.'

'I couldn't agree more.' Chavasse decided to take refuge in as close an approximation to the truth as was possible. 'I suppose I might as well tell all.'

She folded her arms and leaned back in the chair. 'Good, I am waiting.'

'It's quite simple, really. I was on the other side of the bookstall on the station platform at Glasgow looking at the magazines when you bought that map you referred to. I was interested as soon as you mentioned Moidart because that happened to be my destination also.'

'Which doesn't explain how you came by my name?'

He shrugged. 'I had a quick look at the labels on your suitcases when the porter put them on the trolley. Asta Svensson—Glenmore House. Then I checked my own map and discovered that Glenmore is no more than five miles from Ardmurchan Lodge which is leased by my uncle, Colonel Duncan Craig. You know him, I suppose?'

She shook her head. 'This is my first visit to Glenmore, but never mind that now. What happened back there on the mountain? Where did you get to?'

'I climbed the north face. The general idea was that I should be waiting at the summit cairn when you arrived.'

'Ah, I see now,' she said. 'You were caught in the mist.'

'For over an hour, while you kept on walking presumably?'

She nodded. 'And here we are. I was hoping you would get here eventually. I turned my ankle climbing the gate back there on the track.'

'Sorry I was delayed. I saw your light at the same time as our friend turned up.'

She smiled and shook her head. 'Poor Fergus.'

'Was that his name?'

'So he informed me. Fergus Munro. He also told me that I was trespassing and that his employer wouldn't like it—although he followed this with a suggestion that perhaps he didn't need to know.'

'But according to the notice on that gate back there, this is the Glenmore estate.'

'Which is owned by my step-father, Max Donner, the financier,' she said calmly. 'Perhaps you've heard of him?'

'I have indeed. But this raises an interesting situation. Friend Fergus is very probably hot-footing it to Glenmore House at this very moment with his tale of woe. I have a feeling we may expect company in the near future.'

'I sincerely hope so. I haven't the slightest intention of walking any further.'

'I wonder what your step-father will say to the unfortunate Fergus when he discovers who the mystery woman is?'

'I can't wait to see.'

Chavasse took off his raincoat and squatted in front of the fire, hands spread to its warmth and she leaned back in the chair, arms folded beneath her breasts, hair gleaming in the soft lamplight.

'How's your ankle?' he said.

'It could be worse.'

'Shall I take a look at it for you?'

'If you like.'

She peeled off her stocking with a complete lack of embarrassment, and presented a delicately arched foot for his inspection.

The sweep of that long, lovely leg, the curve of the thigh beneath the skirt took the breath out of him. He swallowed hard and glancing up saw the barely suppressed smile.

'Damn you, Asta Svensson,' he said with some passion. 'Play fair or you may get more than you bargained for.'

'Is that a promise?' she replied, the smile breaking through to the surface.

'I should put you over my knee. An attractive proposition, come to think of it.'

'Better and better. We Swedes are reputed to be terribly over-sexed, you know.'

He glanced up sharply and for the moment, her self-assurance seemed to desert her and she became simply a young, nineteen-year-old girl with a rather boyish charm. She smiled shyly, looking down at the hands, folded in her lap and in that one brief moment of revelation he knew she was the most beautiful thing he had ever seen in his life.

He tilted her chin and said wryly: 'You're very lovely, Asta Svensson. So lovely that I think I'd better get back to your foot without further delay.'

Her smile seemed to deepen, to become luminous and she no longer looked shy, but completely sure of herself. She leaned back in the old chair and raised her foot again and Chavasse looked at it, aware of her eyes on him.

There was a faint swelling above the ankle bone beneath a jagged scar. He probed it gently and nodded. 'I don't think it's much. How did you get the scar?'

'Skiing. There was a time when I thought I might make the Olympics.'

'Too bad.' He stood up and took a spare handkerchief from the breast pocket of his tweed jacket. 'I don't think it's much, but a cold-water bandage won't do any harm. I'll take the lamp if I may.'

He left her there in the firelight, went into the kitchen and soaked the handkerchief under the cold tap. When he returned, she was lying back in the chair, eyes closed. The moment he touched her foot, she opened them again.

'Tired?' Chavasse said as he bandaged the foot expertly.

She nodded. 'As the ticket collector said, it was a fair step.'

She mimicked him superbly and Chavasse chuckled. 'It was that and more. Have you had anything to eat?' She shook her head and he produced the remaining half pound of chocolate from his pocket and dropped it into her lap. 'Greater love hath no man. Start on that and I'll see what there is in the kitchen.'

He was back within a couple of minutes. 'Nothing doing, I'm afraid. All the cupboards are locked and the calor gas cylinders are empty, so we couldn't cook anything even if we wanted to.'

'Never mind, the chocolate is fine.' Already half was gone and she held the bar out, a guilty look on her face. 'Have some.'

'That's all right,' he said. 'I had a whole bar to myself back there on the mountain. I'll make do with a cigarette.'

'I must say you seem extraordinarily self-sufficient,' she said. 'What do you do for a living?'

'I'm Lecturer in French Literature at the University of Essex—or at least I will be when the new term starts in October. Something of a return to the fold really.'

'Why do you say that?'

'Oh, I was a university lecturer way back when I first started out, but it all seemed too restricting, so I joined the overseas Civil Service.'

'What went wrong?'

'Nothing really, except that the Empire diminished year by year and they kept moving me on. Kenya, Cyprus, Northern Rhodesia. The future seemed uncertain to say the least, so I decided to get out while the going was good.'

'Back to a calmer more ordered world.'

'Something like that. After all, one doesn't need a great deal. You learn that as you get older. Take this lodge for example. A man could live here quite comfortably.'

'But not alone, surely?'

'All right then, we'll admit Eve into his paradise.'

'But what would they live on in these barren hills?'

'There's fish in the stream, deer in the forest.' He laughed. 'Aren't you familiar with that old Italian proverb? One may live well on bread and kisses?'

'Or chocolate?' she said solemnly, holding up what was left of the bar and they both laughed.

He opened the door and looked out. It was a night to thank God for, the whole earth fresh after the heat of the day and when a bank of cloud rolled away from the moon the loch and the mountains beyond were bathed in a hard white light. The sky was incredibly beautiful with stars strung away to the horizon where the mountains lifted to meet them.

He had not heard her move and yet she spoke at his shoulder. 'We could be the only two people left on earth.'

He turned, aware of her warmth, her closeness, of the eyes shining through the half-darkness and shook his head gently.

'Not for long, Asta Svensson. Not for long. Listen.'

She moved out of the porch and stood there looking down the glen to where the sounds echoed faintly between the hills. 'What is it?'

'A motor vehicle of some description—perhaps two. They'll be here soon.'

She turned and when she moved back inside, her face was quite calm. 'Then let us be ready for them.'

She limped to the fireplace and settled herself into the chair and Chavasse stayed in the porch. A cloud covered the face of the moon for perhaps a full minute and as it moved on, moonlight flooding the glen again, two Land Rovers turned off the track and braked to a halt.

The man who slid from behind the wheel of the first one holding a shotgun was of medium height, thick-set and muscular, his mouth cruel in a pale face. Chavasse recognised him at once from his briefing file. Jack Murdoch, Donner's factor. Fergus Munro came round from the other side of the cab to join him.

Donner was at the wheel of the second vehicle and a woman sat beside him, her face in darkness, a scarf around her head. Probably Ruth Murray, Donner's secretary, Chavasse decided and then Donner got out of the Land Rover and moved to join the others, an enormously powerful looking figure in a sheepskin coat.

Murdoch said something, there was the click of the hammers going back on the shotgun and Donner whistled softly. There was a sudden scramble inside his Land Rover and a black shadow materialised from the darkness to stand beside him in the moonlight.

Chavasse's mouth went dry and fear moved inside him for this was a Doberman Pinscher, the most deadly fighting dog in the world and perfectly capable of killing a man.

'Flush him out, boy! Flush him out!' Donner said softly.

As the dog came forward with a rush, Chavasse stepped out of the darkness to meet it. It froze with incredible control, eyes glowing like hot coals and the growl started somewhere at the back of its throat, carrying with it all the menace in the world.

'That's him, Mr. Donner!' Fergus Munro cried. 'That's the bastard that beat me up and his fancy woman still inside, no doubt.'

Murdoch moved to join Donner, covering Chavasse with the shotgun and Donner looked him over calmly. When he spoke, his Australian origin was plain to the ear.

'This is private property, sport. You should have stayed out.'

There was all the menace in the world in those flat tones and then a tearful, strained voice cut in from the porch. 'Max? Max, is that you? Thank God you're here.'

Donner looked beyond Chavasse, astonishment on his face as Asta Svensson stumbled from the doorway. She started to sway and he ran, moving with incredible speed for such a big man, catching her as she fell.

He looked down at her in amazement and then called quickly: 'Ruth, it's Asta! For God's sake get in here quick,' and hurried inside.

The woman who got out of the Land Rover and crossed to the porch, wore slacks and a sheepskin jacket and was even more attractive in the flesh than Chavasse had expected from her photographs. She looked him over calmly without stopping and went inside.

Fergus Munro turned to Murdoch, a frown on his face. 'And who in the hell is Asta?'

'Something tells me you're in for rather an unpleasant shock, Fergy boy,' Chavasse said pleasantly, and he turned before Fergus could reply and followed Ruth Murray into the lodge, the Doberman at his heels.

Asta was doing very well indeed. She was back in her chair, drinking the glass of water Ruth Murray held for her while Donner leaned over anxiously.

She looked up at him wanly and reached for his hand. 'No, I'll be all right, Max. Really I will. I had a shock, that's all. There was a man here, a horrible man, and then Mr. Chavasse came and threw him out.'

'A man?' Donner said, frowning.

'He threatened me.' Her hand went to her torn blouse. 'In fact he was thoroughly unpleasant.'

Donner straightened slowly, his face very white and there was murder in his eyes as he turned to face Murdoch who stood in the doorway.

'Where's Fergus?'

The roar of an engine breaking into life outside answered him and as he ran out into the porch, one of the Land Rovers drove rapidly away.

'Shall I get after him?' Murdoch demanded.

Donner shook his head, his great hands unclenching slowly. 'No, we'll catch up with him later.' He turned to face Chavasse and held out his hand. 'I'm Max Donner. It would seem I'm considerably in your debt.'

'Chavasse—Paul Chavasse.'

Before Donner could reply, Ruth Murray joined them. 'I think she'll be all right, Max. She's tired more than anything else and she's twisted her ankle.'

'But what was she doing here in the first place? I don't understand.'

'Apparently she was on her way here by train, bought a map, saw there was a track over Ben Breac and thought she'd try it. She wanted to surprise you by just walking in.'

'You mean she's come over that damned mountain this afternoon?' Donner said in amazement.

Ruth Murray nodded. 'I'm not sure where Mr. Chavasse fits in, but he certainly seems to have arrived in the nick of time.'

There was something in her eyes, some cool doubt that had to be met and Chavasse smiled. 'I'm on my way to Ardmurchan Lodge.'

'Colonel Craig's place?' Donner said.

'That's right. He's my uncle. I'm staying with him for a week or two. I was on the same train as Miss Svensson. In fact I noticed her destination from her luggage. When she left the train at Lochside, it seemed strange, so I had a chat with the ticket collector who told me she'd decided to walk over the mountain. He didn't seem to think it was a very good idea. To be perfectly frank, neither did I, so I decided to follow her.'

'And a damned good job too,' Donner said.

Asta appeared in the doorway, smiling weakly. 'I'm terribly sorry, everyone. I'm afraid I made something of a fool of myself. Could we go now, Max? I'm rather tired.'

And as his arm went round her, it was there in the look in his eyes, his instant solicitude, just as Chavasse had guessed from that single photo in the file, that one expression as he had looked up at a sixteen-year-old girl.

'We'll go now, angel,' he said. 'Right now.' He glanced over his shoulder at Chavasse. 'We can drop you off on the way. We pass your uncle's place.'

'That would be fine,' Chavasse said.

Murdoch took the wheel for the drive down the glen, Asta and Donner beside him on the large bench seat, the Doberman at their feet on the floor. Chavasse sat in the rear with Ruth Murray and when the Land Rover swayed on a bend, she leaned against him and smiled.

'The roads aren't quite up to twentieth century standards, Mr. Chavasse. A trifle primitive like everything else in these parts. Will you be staying long?'

'Depends how I like it,' he said. 'I could stay for a month if I wanted. I'm a university lecturer and the term doesn't start until October.'

'Which university?' Donner asked.

'Essex.'

The big man nodded, lapsing into silence again and rain rattled against the windscreen. Ruth Murray smiled. 'Here it comes again. Rain, Mr. Chavasse. Rain and yet more rain and the wind driving in from the Atlantic six days out of seven. I could think of more attractive places for a holiday, but then I suppose it depends what you're looking for.'

'Peace and quiet mainly,' he told her.

Murdoch changed down and swung into a narrow drive through trees with the lights of a house beyond, and braked to a halt. There was a lamp in the porch and lights showed at a window through a chink in drawn curtains, but it was difficult to see much else of Ardmurchan Lodge in the darkness and driving rain.

Chavasse started to get out and Asta turned quickly. 'I hope to get a chance to thank you properly, Mr. Chavasse. Tomorrow perhaps?'

'Plenty of time for that, angel,' Donner told her. 'Let's give Mr. Chavasse a chance to settle in.'

Chavasse got out and as he had expected, Donner followed. 'I'll just see you to the door,' he said and pressed the bell.

Footsteps approached almost at once, the door opened and a greying, military-looking man in a black alpaca jacket peered out. 'Yes, who is it?' he said and then he saw Chavasse and opened the door wide. 'Why, Mr. Paul, we were getting quite worried about you.'

'Hello, George,' Chavasse said briskly. 'You picked up my luggage at Lochailort, did you?'

'We did, sir. The guard gave us your message.'

Chavasse turned to Donner. 'I'd ask you in for a drink, but under the circumstances...'

Donner squeezed his arm. 'I'm the one who'll be supplying the drinks, sport. I'll be in touch.'

He hurried back to the Land Rover. Chavasse stood there, watching it drive away and when he turned, George drew himself stiffly to attention.

'Mr. Chavasse? George Gunn, late Company Sergeant Major, Scots Guards. If you'll come this way, sir. Colonel Craig's waiting in the library.'

CHAPTER SEVEN

COUNCIL OF WAR

COLONEL DUNCAN CRAIG, D.S.O., M.C. AND bar, carried his seventy years well and when he pushed back his chair, stood up and walked to the fireplace, he moved with the physical assurance of a man many years his junior.

He filled his pipe from a tobacco jar and turned to face Chavasse, the lamplight shining in his white hair. 'Have another brandy, my boy. You look as if you could do with it.'

'It *was* rather a long walk,' Chavasse said.

'At least you've accomplished stage one of this operation as I see it, which was to get to know the girl. Under the circumstances, I should imagine we'll be good for a dinner invitation to Donner's place at the very least.'

'You sound as if you're looking forward to the prospect.'

'Eagerly, my boy. Eagerly. There I was, rotting away by inches in Edinburgh with only old George Gunn for company and then Graham Mallory appeared from out of the blue and asked me to go to work again. It's been like a new lease of life, I can tell you. You've read my report?'

'With interest. There seems to be little doubt in your mind that Donner's up to no good, and yet you haven't given a single concrete reason.'

The old man shrugged. 'I spent thirty-five years in Military Intelligence, Chavasse. After a while, you get an instinct for things, a sort of sixth sense that tells you when something isn't quite as it should be. You must know what I mean.'

Chavasse nodded. 'I think I could say it's saved my life on more than one occasion, but I'd still like to hear your reasons.'

At that moment, the door opened and George Gunn came in with the coffee. Colonel Craig accepted a cup and settled himself comfortably into the armchair by the fire.

'To start with, I can't find any real reason for Donner's being here. Oh, he's been out after the deer of course, but the season's very short as you probably know. He hasn't bothered with the grouse at all and he doesn't fish. There just isn't anything else to do in this sort of country and he looks to me to be the last sort of man to want to bury himself in the wilds.'

'How many times have you met him?'

'Half a dozen—no more. He's always been perfectly civil, but he's refused my invitations and hasn't offered any in return. Now that just doesn't make sense, not in a place like this. Another thing—I don't like the kind of people he's surrounded himself with.'

'Who do you mean exactly?'

'Take this fellow Murdoch for a start. I suppose you'll have read his file? He was a captain in a good regiment. Cashiered for embezzlement. I understand he was mixed up in some shady affair in London that ended in a man's death.'

Chavasse nodded. 'He was tried at the Old Bailey for manslaughter five years ago and acquitted. He went to work for Donner almost immediately afterwards.'

'And then his house servants are a rum bunch. When I first moved in, I called to pay my respects. The man who answered the door was as ugly a looking customer as I've ever seen, I'd say he would have been more at home as chucker-out in a waterfront saloon.'

'Was he English?' Chavasse said.

'That's the strange thing. I couldn't tell. You see he never opened his mouth, simply waved me in and disappeared. I waited in the hall and finally Murdoch arrived and told me Donner wasn't in residence which was a lie because I'd seen that plane of his fly in the same morning.'

'So all your meetings with Donner have been purely by chance?'

'No, he called once to ask me not to fish in Loch Dubh.'

'Now this really does interest me,' Chavasse said and he took the ordnance survey map of Moidart from his pocket and spread it out on the table. 'You said in your report that you thought something odd was taking place on an island in the middle of the loch.'

'That's right,' Craig said. 'I was fishing at the lochside one day when some damned rascals Donner has taken on as keepers turned up and escorted me off the estate. They didn't give me much option in the matter either.'

'Who are these people?'

'Old Hector Munro and his sons. They're tinkers—the last remnants of a broken clan. They've wandered the high roads since Culloden, but there's nothing romantic about them, believe me. There's old Hector, Fergus ...'

'Will he be the one I had the run-in with earlier this evening?'

'That's right. He's got one brother—Rory. A big, dark-haired lad and as wild as they come.'

'And you say they ran you off the estate?'

Duncan Craig nodded. 'Fergus knocked George down when he tried to stop them. I wrote a stiff letter of complaint to Donner, mainly because I think it would have looked suspicious if I hadn't. I told him I was considering laying a complaint before the County Constabulary.'

'What happened?'

'He was on my doorstep next morning, smooth as paint, that secretary of his with him to turn on the charm. Now she's a nice lass if you like, though she seems to think the sun shines out of him. Pretty obvious what he keeps her around for.'

'And what did he have to say about Loch Dubh?'

'Gave me some cock and bull story about Arctic Terns nesting in the area and how he didn't want them to be disturbed and he apologised for the Munros. Said he'd kick their backsides and so forth. There wasn't really much I could say. After all, Loch Dubh *is* on his land.'

Chavasse examined the map and George, in the act of clearing the table, paused to point out the loch with a jab of his finger.

'The Black Loch, sir, and black it is, too. About a quarter of a mile wide. That's the island in the centre. There's an old castle there. Built in the fifteenth century by Angus McClaren. Apparently he was known as the Wolf of Moidart.'

'It's ruined, I suppose?'

'Only partially, sir. Myself, I believe he's got someone living out there.'

'I mentioned that in my report,' Craig said.

Chavasse nodded and glanced up at George. 'Why do you think that?'

'The rogue thought he'd have a try for a salmon one night,' Colonel Craig cut in and chuckled. 'With a gaff, you understand. Strictly illegal.'

'I saw a light in the ruins, sir,' George said. 'No doubt about it. And I've seen it since on two other occasions.'

Chavasse turned to Craig. 'What about you?'

Craig shook his head. 'It would certainly explain Donner's anxiety to keep outsiders away.'

Chavasse stood up, crossed to the fireplace and looked down into the flames, a frown on his face. 'But what could be out there, that's the thing?'

Craig shrugged. 'The end of the pipe-line. Perhaps that's where he keeps them before shipping them out.'

Chavasse looked up. 'You know about the latest one of course?'

'This fella Souvorin, the rocket expert?' Craig nodded. 'Yes, there isn't much Mallory hasn't told me.'

'Any sign of his arrival?'

Craig shook his head. 'Impossible to tell. The plane's flown in and out on three separate occasions during the past four days, but it lands on a field behind Glenmore House and it's impossible to get close enough to see anything. Another thing, that damned dog of his roams around the place at will.'

Chavasse nodded. 'It seems as if the island is the place to start, then. At least that was my immediate impression after reading your report.'

'And, just how do you propose to do that?'

'Simple enough with the right equipment. You did pick up my luggage at Lochailort?'

Duncan Craig nodded. 'I was intrigued by that damned great cabin trunk. What have you got in there, for God's sake?'

'Various bits of skin-diving equipment, an aqualung and a collapsible rubber boat.'

'Commando stuff, eh? An assault by night?'

'That's the general idea. But first, I think I'll put my head in the jaws of the tiger, just to see what happens. There's plenty of trout in Loch Dubh, I suppose?'

'Quarter pounders—or occasional pounders—not much else.'

'Good enough for my purpose. I'll borrow a rod if I may and give them a try after breakfast.'

'The Munros will prove unpleasant if they catch you, especially after your bout with Fergus. They don't take kindly to being beaten at anything.'

'Neither do I,' Chavasse said. 'At least I'll get a look at the island and there's nothing like stirring the pot a little. It'll suit me well enough to be dragged off to

Glenmore House as a trespasser. I don't think Asta's going to like that. Donner's going to have to be very nice indeed to make up for the indignity. It might even clinch that dinner invitation you mentioned.'

Craig knocked the ashes from his pipe into the hearth and hesitated. 'What about the girl, by the way? You're sure she isn't mixed up in this?'

Chavasse nodded. 'It's like you said earlier, Colonel Craig. One develops an instinct for this sort of game. She's clean, I'll stake my life on it.'

'No need to sound quite so fervent,' the old man said, 'or is there? Ah well, I'll be able to see her for myself perhaps before very much longer.' He got to his feet. 'Well, I'm for bed, my boy. If you take my advice, you won't be far behind.'

'Ten minutes,' Chavasse said. 'I'm just going to have a last cigarette.'

The door closed behind the old man as he went out and Chavasse got to his feet, crossed to the french windows and drew the curtain. A bare two miles away through the darkness was the loch. Within a few hours he might be in great danger. The rain hammered on the glass, driven by the wind and a sudden spark of excitement moved inside him. He smiled softly, turned and left the room.

On the other side of the hill in his study at Glenmore House, Max Donner sat at his desk, the Admiralty Chart for the Western Isles spread before him. The door opened, and Murdoch came in, unbuttoning a black oilskin coat that streamed with rain.

Donner looked up and leaned back in his chair. 'Well?'

Murdoch shook his head. 'No luck, I'm afraid. That old bastard Hector was as immovable as a rock. Said Fergus had gone off on his evening rounds and they hadn't seen him since. He was lying of course.'

'What did you do?'

'Searched the caravans.' His face wrinkled in distaste at the memory. 'God, if I could only get the stench of them out of my nostrils.'

Donner's hand slammed down hard on the desk. 'I want Fergus, Jack. I want him here where I can get my hands on him, do you understand? My God, when I think of that filthy animal putting his hands on Asta …'

His face became congested and he wrenched at his collar as if he found difficulty in breathing. Murdoch moved to the sideboard, poured whisky into a glass quickly and returned to the desk.

Donner took it down in one easy swallow, then he hurled the glass into the fireplace. 'Right, Jack, you know what to do.'

He leaned over the map again and Murdoch turned towards the door and then hesitated. 'What about Asta, Mr. Donner?'

Donner looked up with a slight frown. 'What do you mean?'

'I should have thought this was just about the worst possible time she could have picked to turn up,' Murdoch said awkwardly. 'I mean, what happens if she notices things she shouldn't?'

'You mind your own damned business,' Donner said coldly. 'I'll look after Asta personally. Now get to hell out of here.'

The door closed softly and Donner sat there at the desk for a moment before getting to his feet and crossing to the fire. He took a cigar from a box on the mantelpiece and lit it carefully, staring down into the flames, thinking about her.

The door clicked open again and the man who entered carrying a tray was taller even than Donner with a scarred, hairless head and a great flat-boned face whose slanted eyes and open nostrils gave him an almost Mongolian cast.

He placed the tray on the desk and turned enquiringly. 'Coffee, Mr. Donner?'

Donner shook his head. 'No, I don't think so, Stavrou. I'll go straight to bed.' He moved to the door, opened it, then he turned and said in Russian: 'Not long now, old friend. Not long.'

He closed the door, crossed the hall and mounted the great staircase. As he turned along the landing, a door opened and Ruth Murray came out. She stood waiting for him, the door behind her slightly ajar.

'How is she?' Donner said eagerly.

'Sleeping like a baby. She'll be fine in the morning.' She put a hand on his sleeve. 'Are you coming to bed?'

He brushed her hand away impatiently. 'Not tonight, Ruth. I've got work to do.' She started to turn and he added quickly, 'Just a minute, there's something I want you to do for me. This man Chavasse. Get on to Essex University. See what you can find out about him.'

'You think he might be an agent?' she said.

'I'm not sure, but one thing's for certain. He handled Fergus too damned competently for any university lecturer. Go on, off you go to bed. I'll see you in the morning.'

Ruth Murray hurried away, filled with a sudden aching fury and when she reached her room, flung herself facedown on the bed in an agony of rage and frustration. The girl—that damned girl. It was just as it always was—the moment she appeared, everything else faded into insignificance. It was as if he had forgotten her very existence.

And Asta, having heard every word of the conversation outside her door, lay very still in her own bed, eyes closed, aware of Donner peering in. And when at last the door closed and his footsteps faded, she reached out to switch on the lamp and sat up, a frown on her face. Suddenly, and for no accountable reason, she was afraid.

CHAPTER EIGHT

THE BROKEN MEN

THE WATERS OF LOCH DUBH WERE as dark as the name suggested, still and calm in the pale, early morning sunshine and on the island in the centre, the grey, broken ramparts of the castle walls lifted above its trees through a faint, pearly mist that drifted across the surface.

There was no sign of life on the island, not that he had expected to see any and he lit a cigarette and took his time over fitting the fishing rod together. Behind him, the heather followed the slope waist-deep to meet the dark line of the trees above him and somewhere a plover called as it lifted into the sky.

A small wind stirred the surface of the water and within moments, small black fins appeared in the shallows where the flies danced. Suddenly, a trout came out of the deep water beyond the sand bar, a good foot into the air and disappeared again.

For the moment forgetting everything else, Chavasse tied the fly Duncan Craig had recommended, apparently one of the old man's own manufacture, and went to work.

Lacking practice, his first dozen casts were poor and inexpert affairs, but gradually, as some of the old skill returned, he had better luck and hooked a couple of quarter-pounders.

The sun was up now and warm on his back. He let out another couple of yards of line, lifted his tip and cast and, out by the end of the sandbank, a triangular black fin sliced through the water.

Two pounds if it was an ounce. His cast, when it came, was the most accurate he had ever made in his life, the fly skimming the surface no more than a couple of feet in front of that black fin. The tail flicked out of the water, the tip of the rod bent over and his line went taut.

His reel whined as the hooked fish made for deep water and he stumbled along the sandbank, playing it carefully. Suddenly, the line went slack and he thought he had lost it, but it was only resting and a moment later, the reel spun again.

He played it for all of ten minutes, moving up and down the sand bar, and in spite of the fact that he wasn't wearing waders, stumbled knee-deep into the water at the end to bring his fish to the landing net.

He turned to wade back on shore, an involuntary smile on his face and a harsh voice said, 'Well and good, me bucko, and a fine dinner we'll make of that.'

The man who had spoken was old—at least seventy, but he stood there in the heather like a rock, a shotgun crooked in his left arm. He wore an old tweed suit, patched many times and white hair showed beneath the dark green glengarry bonnet. His face was the colour of oak, seamed with a thousand wrinkles and covered with an ugly stubble of grey beard.

Behind him, the heather stirred and two men rose to stand at his shoulder. One of them was a tall, well-built lad with ragged black hair and a wild reckless face, his mouth twisted in a perpetual smile. The other was Fergus Munro, still clearly recognisable in spite of the livid bruise down one side of his face, the smashed and swollen mouth.

'That's him, Da, that's him!' he cried, his eyes wild, raising his shotgun waist-high.

'Easy now, Fergus. Easy,' Hector Munro said and moved down the bank to the shore. He paused a couple of feet away from Chavasse and looked him up and down. 'He doesn't look much to me, Fergus,' he said calmly and his right fist swung suddenly.

Chavasse was already turning and it connected in a glancing blow, high on his left cheekbone, the force half spent, but still sufficient to send him flat on his back into the shallows.

He came up on his feet with a rush and the old man's shotgun lifted menacingly. 'Not now, my brave wee mannie. Ye'll get your chance, but not here. Just walk slow and easy before me and mind how ye go or this thing might go off.'

Chavasse held his gaze calmly for a moment, then he shrugged and moved up out of the water and across the beach. 'Have you ever seen the like of that now?' Rory Munro demanded and burst into a gale of laughter.

'Nothing to how he'll look when I've done with him,' Fergus said and as Chavasse passed him, he gave a violent shove that sent him staggering along the path through the heather.

As they topped the hill, Chavasse saw smoke rising on the far side of the trees and heard the voices of children calling to one another at play. So—they weren't taking him to Donner, so much was evident and he realised that he had made a grave miscalculation. At the very least he could expect a bad beating and from the looks of them, neither Rory nor Fergus Munro was the type who knew when to stop.

They skirted the trees and moved down into the hollow containing the camp. The three wagons were old and battered with patched canvas tilts and a depressing air of poverty hung over everything, from the ragged clothes worn by the four women who squatted round the fire drinking tea from old cans, to the bare feet of the half dozen children who played in the far meadow where three bony horses grazed.

Fergus gave Chavasse a push that sent him staggering down the hill into the hollow and the women scattered quickly. Chavasse came to his feet and turned to meet the three men as they followed him.

Hector Munro sat himself on an old box vacated by one of the women, placed his shotgun across his knees and took out a clay pipe. Fergus and Rory moved in to stand on either side of Chavasse.

'An attack on the one of us is an attack on all, Mr. Chavasse, or whatever your name is,' Old Hector began. 'The great pity you weren't knowing that before, now, isn't it?'

'It is indeed,' Chavasse said.

His right elbow sank into Fergus's stomach and he swung to the left, chopping Rory across the right forearm so that he dropped his shotgun with a startled cry of pain. In the same moment, Chavasse turned to run and stumbled headlong as one of the women stuck out her foot.

He rolled desperately to avoid the stamping feet, aware of the women's voices, the stink of their unwashed bodies, old Hector's roar rising above all. And then another voice, strangely familiar, high and clear like a bugle call, lifted into the morning and hooves drummed across the turf.

The women broke and ran and Chavasse staggered to his feet backing against the steps of one of the caravans as Asta Svensson and Max Donner rode down into the hollow. Chavasse was aware of Fergus slipping under one of the caravans, disappearing into the heather like a wraith and then Donner arrived like a descending angel, his face dark with wrath.

The hooves of his horse scattered the fire and he kicked the shotgun from Hector Munro's grasp, a blow from his mount's hindquarters sending the old man staggering. He continued across the hollow and up the other side, reining in sharply, but of Fergus there was no sign.

Asta swung to the ground and ran to Chavasse. She wore cream jodhpurs, leather jacket and white blouse, open at the neck and her hair was plaited into two short pigtails.

'Are you all right, Paul?' she said anxiously, unaware in the excitement of the moment that she had used his first name.

He grinned and held her hands. 'Just fine. I do this sort of thing most mornings. Gives me an appetite for lunch.'

Donner rode into the hollow and reined in his horse. When he looked down at Hector Munro, his face was dark and threatening. 'I told you I wanted that son of yours.'

The old man returned his stare impassively and Donner turned to Chavasse. 'I'm damned sorry about this.'

'He was fishing in the loch,' the old man interrupted. 'Trespassing. We were only obeying your orders.'

'Shut your damned mouth, you rogue,' Donner cried and his riding crop fell across the old man's face.

Munro staggered slightly and looked up with the same calm expression. 'I will remember that, big man.'

'Any more of your damned insolence and I'll have you off my land,' Donner shouted.

'I do not think so, Mr. Donner,' Hector Munro replied.

The riding crop rose again and faltered. For a moment, Donner held the old man's gaze and then he turned his horse, hauling on the bridle viciously.

'For God's sake let's get out of this kennel,' he said and spurred forward.

Chavasse gave Asta a push into the saddle and vaulted up behind her. 'Ready when you are,' he said and she laughed and urged the horse up out of the hollow and across the meadow, passing the children who were chasing each other back towards the camp in full cry.

Donner was waiting for them on the other side of the wood, standing beside his horse smoking a cigarette, the reins looped over his arm.

'Sorry about that,' he said as they rode up. 'If I'd stayed, I might have gone too far. I'm afraid that old goat really had me annoyed.'

Chavasse slid to the ground and moved to meet him. 'My fault, really. If I hadn't gone fishing where I shouldn't, none of this would have happened. Actually my uncle did tell me to stick to the stream, but I didn't think it was all that important.'

Donner looked him over and frowned. 'You're wet through. Better come back to the house with us. I'll fix you up with a change of clothes. You could stay to lunch.'

'That's nice of you,' Chavasse said. 'But I'd rather get back to the lodge. My uncle's promised to introduce me to the finer points of deer stalking this afternoon.'

Donner shrugged. 'All right, make it dinner tonight. Seven-thirty suit you? Of course I'll expect Colonel Craig as well.'

'Fine by me,' Chavasse said.

Donner climbed back into the saddle and Asta said suddenly, 'Deer stalking—that sounds simply marvellous, I don't suppose your uncle would have room for another novice this afternoon, would he?'

Chavasse hesitated, knowing that she would be in the way, and Donner grinned suddenly, as if perfectly aware of his dilemma.

'A good idea, angel. I'm sure Colonel Craig won't mind and I've lots of paper work to get through this afternoon.'

And looking up into her shining face, Chavasse was trapped. 'One o'clock on the dot,' he said, 'and we'll be leaving the lodge on foot.'

'One o'clock it is,' she replied and turned to follow Donner who was already cantering away along the track.

Chavasse reached for a cigarette, but his hand found only a soggy, waterlogged mass. He sighed heavily, turned and started to walk back towards Ardmurchan Lodge. Ah, well, he could still do all that needed to be done that afternoon without her being any the wiser as long as he was careful.

And for a while that afternoon he almost forgot what he had come to this wild, remote place for as they climbed the glen away from the lodge, cutting deep into the hills.

The colonel and George Gunn followed in their own good time and Chavasse and the girl forged ahead, leaving them far behind as they pushed through the heather towards the first great shoulder of the mountain.

She wore a plaid skirt and sleeveless white blouse, a yellow scarf around her hair and as she climbed ahead of him, he was suddenly happy. The air was like wine, the sun warm on their backs and when they reached the top and looked down, the colonel and George seemed very far away.

They moved on and a few minutes later, came over an edge of rock and the mountain fell away before them to the glen below, purple with heather, sweet smelling and beyond, shimmering in the heat haze, the islands were scattered across a calm sea.

The wind folded her skirt about her legs outlining the clean sweep of the limbs and when she pulled off the yellow scarf, the near white hair shimmered in the sun. She fitted the scene perfectly—a golden girl in a golden day and he was suddenly sad, because below in the valley was Loch Dubh, the island in its centre like a grey-green stone, and he had work to do and whatever happened she would be hurt by this affair—that much at least was certain.

'Quite a sight,' he said. 'Let's see if we can spot any deer.'

He took the binoculars from the case which was slung around his neck, focussed them and worked his way carefully across the great slope of the deer forest.

'See anything?' Asta demanded.

There was a sudden movement and a stag moved out of a corrie perhaps a quarter of a mile away and paused in the open. Chavasse pulled Asta close with his free hand. 'Down there by that grey outcrop of rock. Can you see?'

He handed her the binoculars and the breath went out of her in a long sigh. 'I'd no idea they were so handsome. Oh, blast, he's moved out of sight.'

'Probably got wind of us,' Chavasse said. 'From what my uncle was telling me, they can, even at this range.'

She handed the binoculars back and moved to the very edge of the slope and he sat down, his back against a boulder and focussed on Loch Dubh. The grey, broken walls of the old castle sprang into view. There was a square tower at one end, typical of Scottish keeps of the period, which seemed in a reasonable state of repair, but nothing moved.

He followed the shore line carefully, pausing at a wooden jetty. A motor boat was tied up there. As he watched, Jack Murdoch appeared from an arched entrance in the castle wall and walked down through the bushes to the jetty. He dropped into the boat and cast off. Chavasse was aware of the engine, echoing faintly in the valley below and then Murdoch spun the wheel and moved away.

Chavasse lowered the binoculars slowly and when he looked up, saw that Asta had turned and was staring at him, a slight frown on her face. 'Isn't that a motor boat down there on the loch?'

He nodded and got to his feet. 'It certainly looks like it.'

'That's strange,' she said. 'Max told me at lunch that there were terns nesting there this year. That he didn't want them disturbed which was why he's banned the fishing this season. I should have thought a motor boat would have disturbed them even more.'

'Oh, I don't know,' Chavasse said. 'He probably wants to keep an eye on them.'

She still looked dubious and, in a deliberate attempt to steer the conversation away from the dangerous course it had taken, he pointed down the hillside to where a stone hut nestled in a hollow a couple of hundred feet below.

'That'll be the deer stalker's bothy my uncle said we'd make for. Come on— let's see what you're made of.'

He grabbed her hand and plunged down the mountainside and Asta Svensson shrieked in delight as they rushed downwards, stumbling over tussocks, never stopping until they reached the hollow.

They went over the edge, sliding the last few feet and then she lost her balance and fell, dragging Chavasse with her. They rolled over twice and came to rest in the soft cushion of the heather. She lay on her back, breathless with laughter and Chavasse pushed himself up on one elbow to look down at her.

Her laughter faded and in a strangely simple gesture, she reached up and touched his face gently and for one long moment he forgot everything except the colour of that wonderful hair, the scent of her in his nostrils. When they kissed, her body was soft and yielding and she was all sweetness and honey, everything a man could desire.

He rolled on his back and she pushed herself up on one elbow, looking utterly complacent. 'Not unexpected, but very satisfactory.'

'Put it down to the altitude,' he said. 'I'm sorry.'

'I'm not.'

'You should be. I'm fifteen years too old for you.'

'Now that's the English side of you coming out,' she said. 'The only country in Europe where age is presumed to have a dampening effect on love.'

He lit a cigarette without answering and she sighed and leaned over him, a frown on her face. 'Each time we meet I have the same feeling—that somehow, you are in two places at once. Here in person, somewhere else in thought.'

'You're a romantic, that's all,' he said lazily.

'Am I?' she said. 'But this raises limitless possibilities. I can imagine anything I want, for example.'

'Such as?'

'Oh, that you are not what you seem to be. That you followed me over the mountain for a deeper reason than you admitted. That you aren't even a university lecturer.'

'That's licence, not imagination,' he said lightly.

'Oh, but I'm not the only one to think so.'

He turned to look at her sharply and, suddenly, his face was wiped clean of all expression, the face of a stranger. 'And who else indulges in this kind of fantasy?'

'Max,' she said. 'I heard him talking to Ruth last night. He told her to get in touch with Essex University. To check on you.'

Chavasse laughed harshly. 'Perhaps he wonders whether I'm after your money. I don't think he's pleased to see other men in your life.'

She rolled on to her back and stared up into the sky, her face troubled. 'He's over-protective, that's all. Sometimes I think that perhaps I resemble my mother too much for his comfort.'

Chavasse reached out and took her hand gently. 'Are you afraid of him?'

It was a long moment before she replied. 'Yes, I think I am, which is strange, because just as surely, I know he could never hurt me.'

She drew a deep breath and scrambled to her feet. 'But this is nonsense. I came out for the deer-stalking, not psycho-analysis.'

A cry drifted down to them on the warm air and they looked up to see Colonel Craig and George Gunn above them on the shoulder.

'This way, you two,' the old man cried.

She turned to face Chavasse, her face calm and yet there was something very close to an appeal in her eyes and he took her hands in his.

'I would never willingly see you hurt, Asta. Do you believe that?'

Something seemed to go out of her in a long sigh and she leaned against him. 'Oh, I needed to hear that, Paul. You'll never know how much.'

He kissed her gently on the mouth and when they went up the hill, they walked hand in hand.

CHAPTER NINE

NIGHTFALL

BEYOND THE FRENCH WINDOWS, THE BEECH trees above the river were cut out of black cardboard against a sky that was streaked a vivid orange above the mountains. Inside, it was warm and comfortable and Asta in a silk dress of apple green, playing the grand piano softly, was somehow a part of the stillness of the evening just before nightfall.

It was a comfortable room, panelled in oak three centuries old and Donner had had the sense to furnish it in character. The soft light came from a tall standard lamp and a log fire crackled on the wide stone hearth.

Donner, Colonel Craig and Jack Murdoch were in evening wear, but Chavasse wore a beautifully tailored suit of dark worsted that somehow gave him an elegance lacking in the others.

The door opened and Stavrou entered with more coffee. He placed it on the table and Ruth Murray said, 'I'll see to that, Stavrou. You can go.'

He departed as silently as he had come and she got to her feet and moved forward, an attractive figure in a deceptively simple black dress.

'Can I offer you some more coffee, Colonel Craig?' she said.

The old man held up a hand. 'No thanks, my dear, not for me.'

'Another brandy, then?' Donner said.

'Hard to say no. It's the best I've tasted in a long, long time, Mr. Donner.'

'Plenty more where that came from,' Donner said and nodded to Murdoch who got up obediently and reached for the decanter.

Colonel Craig held out his glass. 'And the dinner—remarkable, that's the only word for it. No local cook, I'll be bound.'

Donner chuckled, obviously pleased. 'I should say not. My man Stavrou handles that department. He's Greek and when they're good, they're really good.'

And the dinner had been good, Chavasse had to give him that and leaning on the piano, listening to Asta play, he watched the group by the fire casually.

In any group of people anywhere, large or small, Max Donner would have stood out and Murdoch lounging in the corner, idly fondling the ears of the Doberman sprawled beside his chair, wore his evening clothes with the sort of careless ease to be expected from a man of his background and breeding.

He sipped his drink slowly, staring across the rim of his glass at Ruth Murray who sat beside Colonel Craig on the settee. He wants her, Chavasse thought, but he's too scared of Donner to make any kind of approach.

Ruth Murray held out her glass for the fourth time and Murdoch picked up the decanter and filled it for her. Donner moved forward and in a casual gesture that would have been missed by most people, plucked the glass from her hand.

'You don't look much like a bridge man to me, Colonel,' he said. 'How about a game of billiards? Jack and I play most nights.'

'All right, by me,' the old man said, getting to his feet. 'What about you, Paul?'

Chavasse grinned. 'I'm fine where I am. I don't know where you get the energy from. This afternoon just about finished me off.'

'Suit yourself,' Donner said and he and the other two men went out.

Ruth Murray reached for the brandy decanter and filled another glass. She got to her feet and crossed to the piano. 'I hear you were in the wars again this morning, Mr. Chavasse?'

'A slight misunderstanding,' Chavasse said blandly. 'Nothing more.'

She was a little tight and when she leaned on the piano and spoke to Asta her eyes were full of malice.

'Did you enjoy yourself this afternoon?'

'Tremendously,' Asta said and continued to play. 'You should have come with us, Ruth. It was quite an experience.'

'I'm sure it was.'

'Oh, yes, I learned many things.' Asta stopped playing to tick them off on her fingers. 'That you cannot stalk a stag down-wind, even at a thousand yards.

That I must never hurry. Never attempt to shoot when I am out of breath. Always shoot low if the target is down-hill.'

She paused with a slight frown and Chavasse cut in, 'And never pull the trigger until you're close enough to see the ears move.'

They both burst out laughing and Ruth Murray straightened and said sourly, 'Very funny, I'm sure.'

She went out and as the door closed behind her, Chavasse said, 'I don't think she likes you very much.'

'Not just me,' Asta said. 'Everyone. You see she loves Max and he doesn't love her. It's as simple as that.' She picked up her wrap and draped it over her shoulders. 'Do you mind if we walk for a while? It's a beautiful evening.'

She slipped her arm into his and they went out through the French windows, crossed the terrace and walked through the velvet darkness towards the trees. He lit a cigarette and they leaned on the small bridge over the river.

After a while, she turned, her face a pale blur in the darkness. 'Tell me something about yourself, Paul.'

'What would you like to know?'

'Oh, the really important things. You and your family—where you come from. You're English and yet you're as French as the Pigalle on a Saturday night. Now there's a paradox if you like.'

And he wanted to tell her, that was the strangest thing of all and leaning on the wooden rail of the bridge there in the darkness, he spoke as he hadn't spoken to any other human being in years.

He told of his father killed fighting for France so long ago that it was barely a memory. Of his mother who lived in retirement on that most delightful of all the Channel Islands, Alderney, and of the family farm in Brittany that his wonderful old tyrant of a grandfather still managed so competently.

When they turned to walk back to the house, she hung on to his arm and sighed. 'Life is nothing without roots, that's true, isn't it?'

'We all need a place to rest our heads from time to time,' he said. 'A place where we can be certain of perfect understanding.'

'I wish to God there was such a place for me,' she said and there was a poignancy in her voice that went straight to his heart.

He paused, turning to look down at her and Donner walked out on to the terrace. 'Oh, there you are. Your uncle's ready to leave, Chavasse.'

His voice was calm, but he was angry and Chavasse knew it. Asta ran up the steps and placed a hand on his arm. 'You've lost money, Max. I can always tell.'

He laughed in spite of himself, tucking her arm into his, turning to go inside. 'You can read me like a book, damn you. Yes, Colonel Craig turned out to be just about the handiest man with a cue I've seen in many a long day.'

Duncan Craig already had his coat on when they went inside and stood by the fire, a drink in his hands. There was no sign of Murdoch.

'There you are, Paul. Hope you don't mind if we go now. It's been rather a heavy day and I'm not getting any younger unfortunately.'

'That's all right, uncle.' Chavasse turned to Asta and her step-father. 'Perhaps we can return the hospitality before very long.'

'We'll look forward to that,' Asta said.

Donner cut in quickly. 'Anyway, I'm sure Colonel Craig must be tired.' He took the old man's arm. 'I'll see you to your car.'

Chavasse turned at the door to wave and then he was gone and Asta walked to the fireplace and stared down into the dying embers, suddenly tired. She heard the car start up and move away, there was a quick step in the hall and Donner came in.

She turned to face him, smiling brightly. 'I'm tired myself. Colonel Craig was right. It's been a long day. I think I'll go to bed.'

To her surprise, he didn't argue. 'You look as if you could do with about twelve solid hours,' he said and kissed her on the forehead. 'You go to bed. I'll see you in the morning.'

He walked out into the hall with her and watched her mount the great staircase. When she reached the top and looked back, he was already turning away, moving towards the library door.

As he reached it, the front door opened and Murdoch came in. Donner went to meet him and Asta drew back into the shadows. When they spoke, the voices sounded very clear, but strangely remote in the stillness.

'We've got him,' Murdoch said.

Donner glanced up towards the dark landing and moved closer. 'Where is he?'

'Stavrou's taken him in through the back entrance. Where do you want him?'

'The cellar,' Donner said and his voice sounded cold and hard. 'And don't either of you lay a finger on him. He's my meat. I'll join you in a few minutes.'

Asta hurried along the landing, opened the door and went inside. She leaned against it in the darkness for a moment, trying to collect her thoughts and then she snapped on the light and took off her dress and underskirt quickly.

When she let herself out of the room five minutes later, she was wearing ski-pants, a heavy Norwegian sweater and suede chukka boots. She moved cautiously to the head of the stairs, paused and changing her mind, hurried back along the landing.

A door at the far end gave access to the servants' stairs and she went down quickly, pausing outside the kitchen door. It was then that she first became aware of the noise, faintly in the distance, like some animal in pain and she moved along the corridor and opened the door to the cellars.

The noise rose to meet her, the same strange muffled cries mixed in with the sound of blows. And then it ceased. A moment later, she heard voices and moved back into the corridor. There was a broom cupboard on the other side and she went inside quickly, leaving the door slightly ajar.

The cellar door opened and Murdoch came out looking strangely subdued. Stavrou followed and Donner appeared a moment or two later wiping blood from his hands with a handkerchief. Stavrou closed the door and they all walked away.

Asta waited until their footsteps had faded along the corridor before venturing outside. She felt no fear when she opened the cellar door and went down the steps, because in some strange way, she knew that what she found below would resolve once and for all, the fears and doubts of years.

The light was still on and she moved along a broad white-washed passage that turned into another, off-shoots running into the darkness. She had not been prepared for quite such an extensive system and paused, wondering which way to go. And then she saw blood on the floor.

There was a trail of it, bright splashes that led to a large oak door, its key in the lock. She opened it gently, peered into darkness, then fumbled for the light switch.

The man who hung by his wrists from a hook in the ceiling was Fergus Munro, she was able to tell that much, but only just. The blood from his broken body had gathered into a pool beneath his feet and one look at the ghastly eyes, fixed for all eternity, told her that he was dead.

And again she was strangely calm, knowing only that she had to get out of that place, leaving all as she had found it. Get out and go to Paul at Ardmurchan Lodge.

She locked the door quickly, went back along the passage and mounted the steps. All was quiet as she moved past the kitchen, opened the back door and let herself out. She hurried across to the garage and then paused. If she took one of the Land Rovers they would hear her leave. She hesitated and then remembered the old bicycle she had seen Jack Murdoch using about the place. She found it leaning against a bench at the back of the garage and wheeled it outside quickly. A moment later, she was riding away through the darkness.

It was all of five miles to Ardmurchan Lodge, but the road was surprisingly good and the full moon gave her perfect visibility. It was little more than half an hour later that she topped a small rise and looked down at the lodge in the hollow below.

There was a light at the rear where French windows stood open to the terrace and when she rode in through the front gate, she parked the bicycle against a tree and walked round.

As she turned the corner, she drew back sharply into the shadows. Chavasse had moved out on to the terrace wearing a black rubber skin-diving suit, the hood giving him a strangely medieval appearance. There was a rucksack on his back and he carried a large canvas grip in one hand.

Colonel Craig moved out and clapped him on the shoulder. 'Good luck, my boy, and don't try to win the war on your own. All we need is some conclusive proof, remember.'

Chavasse smiled once, turned and moved away across the lawn and the old man went back inside and closed the French windows. Asta waited until he pulled the curtains, cutting off all light and then went after Chavasse, silent on crepe soles.

CHAPTER TEN

DARK WATERS

CHAVASSE COVERED THE TWO MILES FROM the lodge to the loch in exactly twenty minutes, following the track beside the river, clear in the moonlight. Already the weather was changing and when he looked beyond the mountains, a blanket of dark moved in from the sea snuffing out the stars one by one. All he needed now was a little rain for conditions to be near perfect and with luck he might even get that before very long.

He moved away from the river as he neared the loch, cutting across the moor to drop down into the quiet bay from which he had fished that morning. The moon still shone brightly and he put down the canvas grip, took off his rucksack and crouched on the edge of the water, looking out towards the island.

The north end was the place to make a landing, rocks and sandbanks scattered over a wide area, bushes growing down to the shoreline. He marked it well and as clouds started to pass across the face of the moon, turned and set to work.

He opened the rucksack and took out the aqualung that he might or might not need, depending on what happened. The collapsible boat came next. He took it out of the canvas grip, activated the compression cylinders and the boat started to inflate with a soft hiss.

He had been aware of the movement in the heather behind him for at least two full minutes and when he turned and jumped into darkness, it was with the speed of a tiger. His hands gripped soft flesh savagely and Asta gasped his name.

'Paul! Paul, it's me!'

A cloud moved away from the face of the moon and he gazed down at her for a moment and then sat back, squatting on his haunches as darkness descended and rain began to fall.

'All right, Asta,' he said calmly. 'I think you'd better start talking.'

'Max killed Fergus tonight,' she said flatly.

'Where?'

'Back at the house. The body's still there in the cellar, hanging from a hook like an animal. He beat him to death, Paul.'

'Does he know you saw him?'

She shook her head. 'I slipped away quietly, took Murdoch's bicycle from the garage and rode over to Ardmurchan Lodge to you.'

'And arrived just as I was leaving?'

'That's right.' She gripped his arm and leaned forward, her face a pale blur. 'Tell me, Paul. Tell everything! I must know!'

He had little choice and knowing that he took her hands and held them tightly. 'All right, angel. You asked for it. I'm a NATO Intelligence agent and your step-father and his friends are working for the other side, it's as simple as that.'

Her hands tightened in his and then suddenly she fell forward against him. He gave her only a moment and raised her chin with a finger. 'Whose side are you on, Asta?'

She gripped his arms fiercely and gave him a little shake. 'Damn you, Paul Chavasse, do you need to ask?'

The hissing stopped behind them as the compression bottles emptied themselves and he stood up. 'Where are you going—the island?'

'That's right. Donner's up to something out there and I'd like to know what it is.'

'I thought so. I knew that's what you were watching this afternoon on the hillside through the binoculars. Can I come with you?' Before he could protest she went on, 'I might as well wait for you in the boat as here on the shore.'

'All right,' he said, 'but no nonsense when we get there and you do exactly as you're told.'

She settled herself into the prow with the aqualung and he pushed off and scrambled into the stern. The moon was completely obscured by cloud and a thin rain was falling as he paddled in a wide circle that carried them into the path of the emptying river so that the current swept them in towards the northern point of the island.

Asta leaned over the prow, fending off the rocks and, when they grounded on a bank of sand and shingle, Chavasse scrambled over into the shallows, and ran the boat into the shelter of overhanging bushes.

'Now wait here,' he whispered. 'I shouldn't be very long. If you hear any kind of fuss at all, cast off, paddle back to the beach and get to Ardmurchan Lodge as quickly as you can. Colonel Craig will know what to do.' She opened her mouth to protest and he closed it firmly with one hand. 'No arguments. If the worst comes to the worst, I can swim for it. Now be a good girl.'

He splashed through the shallows, following the shoreline before cutting up through the bushes to the base of the castle wall. At this point, it was crumbling badly and he pushed his way through a wasteland of nettles, scrambling across a jumbled mass of broken stones to a point where he could see inside.

The walls formed a rectangle enclosing a paved courtyard. There was a roofless building to his right and a line of half ruined pillars stretching towards the arched gateway.

To his left, the tower of the keep lifted squarely into the night, dark and silent and he moved towards it, mounting stone steps to the battlements. At this end of the building, the walls seemed to be almost intact and where they joined the tower, there was a broad rampart and two decaying cannon still at their stations.

He peered over the edge and saw water breaking in white spray over jagged rocks forty feet below. He turned to examine the tower. It raised its head another twenty feet into the night and he stiffened suddenly. There was a light showing from the window near the top, only the merest chink as if a curtain had been carelessly drawn, probably not even visible from the shore.

A crumbling buttress made a natural ladder, but as he moved towards it, the silence was shattered by the sound of an engine breaking into life on the far side of the loch and the motor boat moved towards the island.

Chavasse hurried across to the wall and a couple of minutes later, the engine was cut and the boat drifted in. He couldn't see the jetty from that point, but he heard the sound of the landing, and the scrape of a shoe on stone.

He moved cautiously back along the battlements, crouching in a corner of darkness where the tower joined the wall and peered down. Two men crossed the courtyard talking in low voices. They paused directly beneath him and opened a door in the base of the tower. It was Donner and Murdoch. As a brief shaft of light fell across the flagstones he saw them clearly and then the door closed again.

He descended the stone steps to the courtyard and moved towards the tower, keeping to the shadow of the wall. He could hear voices, a low murmur that sounded as if it was coming from somewhere beneath him. He listened carefully at the door for a moment, then opened it gently.

An oil lamp stood in a niche, briefly illuminating a dank stone chamber whose walls glistened with moisture. To his right, circular stone stairs lifted into the darkness. To his left, another door stood open slightly. The voices were coming from inside.

He pushed it open an inch or two at a time. There was a stone landing, then the beginning of some steps, dropping away to his left. The roof was supported by ribbed vaulting, he could see that, and then someone crossed his narrow angle of vision and paused to light a cigarette.

He wore the grey-green uniform of a private in the German Army, his face a dark shadow under the peak of the combat cap. The sight was so unreal, so unexpected, that Chavasse momentarily closed his eyes. When he opened them again, the man had gone.

He pushed open the door a little further and crawled inside on his stomach, peering cautiously over the edge of the landing. The room below was large, iron, military-style beds ranged around the stone walls. Max Donner leaned over the table in the centre, Murdoch at his side, a map spread out before them and the men who crowded round him all wore German Army uniform, except for two who were in British Army battledress.

The voices were a low murmur and then one of the men spoke as if asking a question. Donner laughed harshly and when he replied, Chavasse could hear him clearly.

'It's all taken care of. Nothing can possibly go wrong. Now let's have a drink and then we'll go over it again.'

Chavasse backed out slowly, closing the door behind him and stood up. Now that his eyes had become accustomed to the half-light he could see that above his head, the spiral stone staircase halted at a wooden door. Remembering the light from the room above, he went up the stairs quickly and tried the handle, but it was locked.

But someone was up there, so much was evident. Someone who had to be kept under lock and key, which was interesting. He let himself out into the courtyard, crossed to the steps and went up on to the battlements quickly.

When he reached the rampart beneath the tower, the chink of light still showed clearly from the window above his head and he started to climb the buttress, taking care where he placed his weight on the crumbling surface.

The window was barred and a glass casement had been fitted inside. He crouched down, hanging on to the bars and peered through a narrow gap where the drawn curtain had failed to join.

At first he could see little of interest. Stone walls, the end of a bed and then he changed his angle and excitement surged through him. The man who sat at the table in the centre of the room reading by the light of an oil lamp was Boris Souvorin. There was no doubt about it, Chavasse had been shown too many photographs of the man to be mistaken.

He reached through the bars and tapped on the window. Souvorin sat up at once, a startled expression on his face. Chavasse tapped again and the Russian glanced towards the window. He put down his book and crossed the room slowly.

When he pulled the curtain and found Chavasse peering in at him, he recoiled, fear on his face. Chavasse made an urgent gesture. The Russian hesitated, then he opened the casement.

'Who are you? What do you want?' he said in a whisper.

'My name is Chavasse. I'm a NATO Intelligence agent. You're Boris Souvorin.'

'You're here to help me?' Souvorin gripped the bars tightly. 'Thank God. The past few days have been a waking nightmare. Can you get me out?'

'Not right now. Your host, Max Donner, is down below holding some kind of briefing with a group of men, dressed in the main as soldiers of the Federal Republic of West Germany. Have you any idea what he's up to?'

'None at all.' Souvorin shook his head. 'They brought me here three days ago and I haven't been out of this room since. Where is this place?'

'Moidart—the North-West coast of Scotland. One of the loneliest spots in the British Isles. Has he told you what he intends to do with you?'

'I am to be taken to Russia and soon. He was very certain of that when he spoke to me.'

'Right,' Chavasse said. 'I'll have to go now, but don't worry. I'll be back. They're not going to take you anywhere you don't want to go.'

Souvorin closed the window and as the curtains were pulled across, Chavasse went back down the buttress. He hurried along the battlements, went down the steps and crossed to the gap in the wall.

It was raining quite hard now, falling through the darkness with a violent rush that killed all sound and disregarding caution, he ran through the bushes and splashed along the shore. He found the boat at once, but there was no sign of Asta and then she moved out of the darkness to join him.

'Where in the hell were you?' he demanded savagely.

'Sheltering under a tree from the rain,' she said. 'It's been pretty foul waiting here. I'm soaked to the skin.'

She got into the boat and he pushed it out into deep water and scrambled over the stern. At the same moment the engine of the motor boat coughed into life. Chavasse waited, listening to its sound fade across the loch, then he started to paddle.

Asta leaned forward. 'I was beginning to get worried. When the motor boat turned up, I didn't know what to think. Who was it?'

'Your step-father and Murdoch. They've got a bunch of goons in the basement of the tower dressed as German soldiers.'

'But why?'

'God knows. The only thing I know for certain is that Boris Souvorin, a Russian rocket engineer who's been working for the British Government and who disappeared from his home a week ago, is locked in the room at the top of the tower, awaiting a quick passage to Russia.'

She drew in her breath sharply. 'You're sure of this?'

He nodded. 'I've just been talking to him. Unfortunately his window was barred and I couldn't very well take on the whole crew single-handed.'

'What are you going to do?'

'I'll get back to Ardmurchan Lodge as quickly as possible, but it'll take time to get in touch with my people—set things in motion and so forth.'

'Can I help?'

He hesitated, but it had to be said. 'You could, you could help a lot. You see it's unlikely that we'll be ready to move in on Donner before tomorrow and whatever happens, I don't want him to suspect that there's anything wrong before then.'

'And you'd like me to go back to Glenmore House as if nothing had happened?'

'I hate asking you,' he said. 'But if Donner finds you missing, he's bound to start looking for you. That could upset everything.'

The boat grounded and he went over the side and dragged it up on to the sand. She stepped out and turned to face him. 'I'd better be off then,' she said calmly. 'I think I can get back in without being seen.'

Chavasse unzipped the front of his rubber suit and took out a Smith & Wesson .38 magnum. 'Take this. I don't know if you've ever used one, but it might come in handy.'

She reached up to kiss him and then she was gone like a shadow into the curtain of rain. He stood looking after her for a moment and then he dragged the boat off the sandbar and pushed it out of sight under the bushes. He left the aqualung inside so that he had no weight to carry and started to run, following the shore towards the point where the river emptied into the loch.

He found the path and ran along it, brushing through ferns heavy with the rain. Whatever else happened now, speed was essential.

Somewhere thunder rumbled and beyond the mountains, sheet lightning flickered across the sky and then the rain increased into a solid monsoon-like downpour that killed all sound, dashing against his face with icy force.

When he came over the edge of the hollow fifteen minutes later and looked down at the lodge, it lay in darkness except for a thin streak of light showing at the French windows to the terrace at the rear.

He came out of the wood, opened the wicket gate in the wall and hurried across the lawn. The French window stood open slightly, the velvet curtain lifting as the rain drove against it.

He pushed open the window and stepped inside. The lamp on the table was out, but the room was illuminated by the light from the blazing log fire. Flames flickered across the oak-beamed ceiling, casting fantastic shadows that writhed and twisted constantly and the whisky in the glass on the small table beside Colonel Craig in his wing-backed chair, gleamed amber and gold.

Chavasse took a step towards him and stumbled, falling to one knee. George Gunn lay sprawled beside the table, eyes fixed and staring, the head turned so far to one side that it could only mean that his neck was broken.

And Craig was just as dead. The only thing that kept him upright in the chair was the cord which had choked life out of him. It would have needed strength to kill a man like that—real strength.

Chavasse turned, sick at heart, and Donner came in from the hall, a Lüger in his hand. They looked at each other for a long moment and Donner laughed harshly, but it was the man at his shoulder who did the talking.

'So we meet again, Mr. Chavasse?' Boris Souvorin said pleasantly. 'Did you have an enjoyable swim?'

CHAPTER ELEVEN

FIREBIRD

THE SOUND OF THE LAND ROVER slowing to a halt outside pulled Asta back to reality just as she was dropping off to sleep. She threw back the bedclothes, ran across to the window in time to see her step-father and a stranger, hurry up the steps into the porch. They were followed by Paul Chavasse, Stavrou and Murdoch a pace or two behind.

Asta dropped the curtain, went across to the door and opened it. The landing was in darkness and she tip-toed along to the end and peered over the banisters.

They were standing in a group in the hall below and Chavasse in whipcord slacks and a white polo-necked sweater, seemed completely relaxed, that slight inimitable smile on his face. For a moment she thought everything was all right and then she noticed the revolver Stavrou was holding.

When Donner spoke, she could hear him perfectly. 'Put him in the cellar for half an hour,' he told Stavrou. 'We'll have words later.'

The library door closed and Stavrou and Chavasse moved away. Asta stayed there, gripping the banister rail with both hands.

'So they've picked up your boyfriend, have they?'

The voice was unnaturally loud in the stillness and when she turned, Ruth Murray was standing no more than a yard away, swaying drunkenly, a glass in one hand, a decanter in the other.

Asta brushed past her and went back to her room. She closed the door behind her, but it was opened again almost immediately and Ruth entered.

'Why don't you go to bed?' Asta said patiently. 'I'm not in the mood.'

'But maybe I am,' Ruth said. 'Maybe I'm in the mood for a lot of things. Truth or consequences for instance.' She put the decanter down carefully and went into the bathroom. When she came out, she was holding the rain-soaked sweater that Asta had worn earlier. 'You've really been having yourself a ball, haven't you, and don't bother to deny it. I saw you come in. I wonder what Max would say?'

'You can always try him.'

Ruth's foolish smile disappeared and in a moment her face was contorted with fury. 'You think you're so damned good, don't you? That all you have to do is whistle and he'll come running. Well I could tell you a thing or two about Mr. Max Donner.'

'You'd be wasting your time.'

'Is that so? Just like your mother. She thought she knew how to handle him and look where it got her.'

When she carried on, it was as if she was talking to herself. 'Everything had to be just right, so they told him to get a wife. A nice normal wife. That's why he married your mother.' She tossed back the contents of her glass and refilled it, brandy slopping to the floor. 'The bloody fool. She found out about him. She found out about the great Max Donner. He couldn't have that, now could he?'

'What are you trying to say?' Asta demanded, and something moved coldly inside her.

'Remember how your mother died? Skin-diving off Lesbos?'

'That's right. She went too deep. Ran out of air.'

Ruth Murray laughed harshly. 'What would you say if I told you her emergency cylinder was empty to start with?'

Asta clutched at the end of the bed to steady herself. 'What are you trying to say?' she said in a whisper.

'What do you think I'm trying to say?' Ruth Murray emptied the last of the brandy into her glass and took it down in one quick swallow. 'Yes, he's quite a man, our Max, or Ivan or Boris or Anton or whatever his damned name is.'

Asta managed to make it to the bathroom before she was sick, leaning over the basin, her whole body retching. And when she finished, a stranger stared out at her from the mirror, eyes burning in a face that was the same colour as the hair.

When she returned to the bedroom, Ruth Murray lay on her back sleeping peacefully. Asta looked down at her for a moment, then she got another pair of slacks and a sweater from the wardrobe and dressed quickly. The revolver

Chavasse had given her was beneath her pillow. She slipped it into her pocket and went out.

There was only one thing she was certain of—that she was going to kill Max Donner. She moved along the landing and as she reached the stairhead, Chavasse crossed the hall to the library, Stavrou at his back with a gun. They went inside, Asta drew back into the shadows and waited.

Donner was standing at the fireplace smoking a cigar when Chavasse and Stavrou went into the library. There was no sign of Souvorin or Murdoch.

He looked Chavasse over carefully for a moment and then nodded. 'All right, sport. I'm a busy man and my time's limited, so let's get down to business.'

'A long way from Rum Jungle,' Chavasse said in Russian.

Stavrou grunted, moving in quickly, but Donner held up a hand, his face calm. 'You seem to know more than I thought you did.'

'Clay Crossing in 1933 till you joined up at Kalgoorlie in 1939,' Chavasse said. 'Six years of nothing in between and don't tell me you were going walkabout in the bush.' He helped himself to a cigarette from a silver box on the table. 'Whatever happened to Donner by the way? He must have been really perfect. Austrian immigrant, orphaned, no relatives.'

'He stowed away on a Russian freighter in Sydney Harbour in 1933.'

'Bound for the land of milk and honey?'

'He did all right,' Donner said. 'He had everything he needed.'

'And in return you took everything he had—everything that was Max Donner.'

'What put you on to me?'

Chavasse shrugged. 'The same sort of thing that pulled Gordon Lonsdale down. In the end you have to depend on others. Little people who aren't quite as clever as you are, like that stupid little Admiralty clerk, Simmons, and Ranesvsky.'

'What about Ranevsky?'

'He paid Simmons in new notes. They not only led us to Ranevsky—they also provided us with the interesting fact that he'd cashed a cheque signed by you.'

'That wouldn't get you very far.'

'No—it wasn't even worth mentioning at the trial, but it did start us checking and that was all that was needed, especially when the trail went all the way back to six blank years.'

'Not to worry,' Donner grinned. 'I've had a good run and I'll be out of it soon. One last big coup, that's all.'

'Don't kid yourself,' Chavasse said. 'You're not going anywhere.'

'A good try,' Donner said, 'but it won't work. Craig's man, George Gunn, told me everything I needed to know back there at the lodge.'

'I don't believe you,' Chavasse said.

'All right, try this for size. You're only up here on the snoop to see what I'm up to and Craig was supposed to provide a cover.' He grinned. 'I'm forgetting the most important bit. Nobody makes a move till you report back so I've got all the time in the world.'

For a moment, all that Chavasse felt showed clearly on his face. 'Don't take it to heart, sport. You haven't seen Stavrou in action. George Gunn was a tough bird. He only spilled his guts because he thought it would save the old man's skin.' Donner laughed harshly. 'He was wrong.'

He stood there, a strange, expectant look on his face as if he was waiting for something and Chavasse, fighting with every fibre of his being the overwhelming desire to fling himself forward to destroy this man, helped himself to another cigarette and lit it, hands shaking slightly.

When he spoke, his voice was quite calm. 'That's the way it goes sometimes.'

Donner laughed delightedly. 'You know, I like you, sport. You've got class. I think I'll take you back with me. I bet they could squeeze a lot of good stuff out of you.'

'I'll say this,' Chavasse told him. 'You certainly had everyone fooled with this Souvorin business. When he defected, he was accepted without question. He's spent the best part of a year working in the classified section of the Rocket Research Establishment, Boscombe Down.'

'That was the general idea. What he's taking back home in his head alone should set your people back five years at least. If it comes to that, what I'm taking home should put you out of the race altogether.'

For a moment, the monumental ego of the man broke through to the surface and Chavasse seized on it quickly. 'I was wondering about that. I realised it had to be something pretty special when I caught a glimpse of your private army back there on the island.'

'You'd never guess, sport. You'd never guess in a thousand years.' With a sudden gesture, Donner tossed the cigar into the fire. 'What the hell—why not?'

He crossed to a door in the far corner, opened it and disappeared. He was back in a moment, pulling on a German Army officer's tunic which had obviously been made to measure. 'Perfect fit, isn't it?' he said as he buttoned it up.

Chavasse took in the badges of rank, the insignia, the triple row of medal ribbons. 'You must have had a hard war. I see you've got everything that counts including the Knight's Cross.'

'And they didn't give *that* away with the rations.' Donner clicked his heels. 'Allow me to introduce myself. Colonel Gunther von Bayern, German Military Intelligence on temporary detachment to the Royal Artillery on the island of Fhada in the Outer Hebrides.'

'Fhada?' Chavasse said, frowning. 'That's a Missile Training Base.'

'It sure is, sport. Did you think I was joking?' Donner shook his head. 'Von Bayern and a detachment of nine men from the German 101st Missile Regiment are flying in to Glasgow airport in the morning. They then proceed by road to Mallaig where a tank landing craft will be waiting to run them across to Fhada.'

And then Chavasse saw everything. 'Let me guess. They won't even get as far as Mallaig. You're going to work a switch.'

'Let's say we divert them to here and then take over. There are thirty-eight men stationed on Fhada. I shouldn't think we'll have too much trouble. They'll be under wraps before they know what's hit them.'

'There must be something pretty special there to make a stunt like this worthwhile.'

'You could say that. You British never change, do you? The Empire crumbles, the pound totters, you cut back on defence and while everyone gloats, you get together with the Germans on a nice little mutual research programme that no one else knows a damn thing about.'

'Such as?'

'A new kind of rocket propulsion unit that produces limitless power from a negative energy field, whatever that's supposed to mean. It's being tried out in a new anti-tank missile called Firebird. That's what von Bayern and his boys are here for—to train on the operational side.'

'I suppose Souvorin put you on to this?'

Donner nodded. 'And he's going in with us, too, just to make sure we collect the right item.'

Chavasse shook his head. 'You'll never get away with it.'

'Why not? Once we take over, all we need is five hours. On the right signal, a fast diesel trawler comes in and takes off the missile and the men. She sails under the Panamanian flag, by the way. Once she's out to sea again, she's just one more trawler amongst the hundreds that fish those waters from every country in Europe.'

Chavasse, searching desperately for a flaw, clutched at the only straw in sight. 'There's standard checking procedure between Guided Weapon H.Q. and all outstations. If they get radio silence from Fhada, they'll want to know why.'

'But they won't. We'll maintain essential radio contact until we leave and emergency checking procedures don't come into operation until radio silence has lasted for six hours. That gives us plenty of time to move on. Anything else?'

Chavasse shook his head slowly. 'You seem to have thought of just about everything.'

Donner laughed. 'Don't worry, sport, Stavrou will take good care of you while I'm gone and when I come back, we'll fly out of here together. Back to the dear old homeland.'

'Does Asta come too.'

'Where I go, Asta goes from now on.'

'I wonder what she'll have to say about that.'

Donner's face hardened. 'She'll do as she's told because, like you, she isn't going to have much choice in the matter.' He nodded to Stavrou. 'Go on, take him below. I've wasted enough time.'

He turned abruptly and went into the other room, unbuttoning his tunic and Stavrou touched Chavasse gently on the back of the neck with the barrel of his revolver.

It was cold on the way through the hall, colder still in the dimly lit passages beneath the old house. The cellar outside which they stopped had a gnarled oak door, secured by an iron bar fitted into sockets on either side.

Stavrou stood well away and nodded and Chavasse raised the bar. He weighed it in both hands for a moment longer than was necessary and Stavrou took careful aim and thumbed back the hammer of his revolver.

Chavasse grinned. 'All right, you bastard, I get the point.'

He dropped the bar on the ground and went inside. The door closed behind him and the bar clanged into place.

He listened to the man's steps recede along the corridor, then turned to examine the cellar. It was almost totally dark, a patch of light showing from a tiny barred window on the other side. Rain drifted in through a hole in the glass and when he pulled himself up, he looked out at ground level across the courtyard to the stables and the garage.

He dropped to the ground and went right round the room, feeling at the walls, but there was no way out—not even a possibility of one—and he squatted in the corner by the door, and waited.

He dozed fitfully and was finally awakened by the sound of footsteps in the courtyard. He got to his feet and hurried across to the window. The first grey light of dawn seeped through and he looked outside in time to see one of the Land Rovers turn out of the garage, Jack Murdoch at the wheel. He was followed by Donner and Souvorin in the other, Donner driving.

He wondered where they were going? To the loch probably, to pick up the rest of the party. Then to the appointed place on the Mallaig road to wait in ambush for von Bayern and his men.

He dropped to the floor and slammed the heel of his hand in impotent rage against the wall. The wheels were turning, the whole damned thing was in motion and there was nothing he could do about it.

He slumped down against the wall, his hands tucked into his armpits, trying to keep warm in the intense cold. It was perhaps half an hour later that he heard slow, cautious footsteps approaching along the passage outside. A door was opened and then another. Chavasse got to his feet, drew back against the wall and waited.

The steps paused outside, the bar was lifted and then the door opened. He raised his fist to strike and Asta stepped into the room.

CHAPTER TWELVE

RUN TO THE MOUNTAIN

SHE WAS TREMBLING AS HE HELD her in his arms and when she looked up, her face was pale in the dim light. 'I forgot and went into the next cell. Fergus is still there.' She shuddered. 'Stavrou's in the kitchen, but Max and the others have gone.'

Chavasse nodded. 'Yes, I saw them leave from the window.'

'I saw them bring you here during the night,' she said. 'What happened?'

'They were waiting for me when I got back to the lodge. I'm afraid I made a bad mistake. Souvorin wasn't what I thought he was.'

'What about Colonel Craig and George?'

'Stavrou killed them both.'

Her eyes widened in horror and she swayed slightly. He held her for a while, her head against his chest. When she looked up, her voice seemed unnaturally calm.

'It's Max who's to blame, isn't it, Paul? Stavrou's just a blunt instrument. He murdered my mother, did you know that?'

Chavasse shook his head. 'Not for certain, but I read the accounts of the accident in his file and it always seemed a possibility. How did you find out?'

'Ruth told me last night. She was so drunk, I don't think she really knew what she was saying.' She moved to the window and stared up at the grey light. 'I wanted to kill him, Paul. I sat on the landing in the darkness waiting for him to come out of the library and then I thought about what might happen to you.' She took the Smith & Wesson out of her pocket. 'You'd better have this back.'

He checked the gun quickly and slipped it into his belt. 'You say Stavrou's in the kitchen?'

'That's right. I think he's having breakfast. What's Max up to, Paul? Where has he gone?'

He told her everything in a few brief sentences and when he had finished, she nodded, looking strangely grave. 'Surely there's something we can do? He must be stopped.'

'He will be if I've got anything to do with it,' Chavasse said. 'Where's the nearest telephone—the library?'

'There isn't one,' she said.

'Are you sure?'

She nodded. 'I thought it was strange, but when I mentioned it to Max yesterday, he said he was here for peace and quiet, not to have the phone ringing at all hours.'

'Is there any other vehicle in the garage besides the two Land Rovers?'

She shook her head. 'Not a thing. Why?'

'Oh, I had a wild idea that somehow we might have reached the Mallaig road in time to warn those Germans about Donner's ambush.'

She frowned slightly. 'Isn't the road to Mallaig in the next valley?'

'That's right.'

'Then the only way to get there would be to drive to the head of the glen and go through the pass. That must be all of ten miles.'

'What are you getting at?'

'Wouldn't it be quicker to go over the top on foot?'

Excitement and hope surged through him and he grabbed her hand. 'I'm not sure, but we can have a damned good try.'

When he opened the door to the passage which led to the kitchens, it was still and quiet, but somewhere there was a sudden scratching and the dog whined. Chavasse pushed Asta along the passage quickly and they went out into the courtyard.

It was beginning to rain again and the top of the great ridge which divided the two glens was covered in mist. They went round the side of the house to the lawn at the rear and crossed the bridge over the stream.

On the other side, the path lifted steeply through a small wood, emerging into a heather-covered clearing perhaps fifty yards across, the slopes beyond covered with pine and alder trees. Below them was the panorama of the valley,

Glenmore House beside the stream and beyond it the meadow Donner used as an airstrip, the red and silver Beaver parked at one end.

As Chavasse and Asta came out of the wood into the clearing, Hector and Rory Munro moved out of the trees some twenty or thirty yards to the right. The old man carried a brace of pheasant and his shotgun was tucked under his arm. Chavasse caught Asta's arm to pull her back, but he was too late.

The Munros stood quite still, looking down the slope towards them and Chavasse said in a low voice, 'Ignore them—just keep going. No reason why they should interfere.'

And then a cry lifted high in the morning air and when they turned and looked down to the house, Stavrou was standing in the courtyard looking up towards them, the Doberman straining at its leash.

'Stop them!' he called. 'Bring them back!'

At the same moment, one of the Land Rovers turned into the courtyard, braked to a halt and Donner jumped out.

Hector Munro dropped the pheasants and both he and his son reached into their pockets for cartridges. Chavasse pulled out the Smith & Wesson and fired once, high above their heads, sending them back into cover.

He urged Asta across the clearing and as they reached the shelter of the trees, lead shot whispered through the branches and below, in the courtyard, the Doberman gave an unearthly howl as Stavrou slipped its leash.

They started to run, following the slope, pushing upwards through dripping ferns until they emerged on to a wide, boulder-strewn plateau. A few yards away, a track swung east, climbing the slope of the great hog's-back in a gradual curve.

Asta started forward and Chavasse grabbed her arm. 'We wouldn't get a quarter of a mile before that damned dog caught up with us. How's your climbing?'

'Only fair.'

'That'll have to do. Come on.'

On the far side of the plateau, the slope was volcanic in origin, split and fissured into great blocks of stone forming a giant's staircase. Chavasse ran towards it, Asta at his heels and as they reached the first tilt of stone, the Doberman came over the edge of the plateau behind them.

It barely paused before rushing on, snaking between the boulders and Chavasse pushed Asta ahead of him. 'Get going,' he said. 'You've got about two minutes to climb beyond his reach.'

That first slope was gentle enough and he knew with heart-stopping certainty that the dog would have no trouble in scaling it either. They scrambled over great blocks of stone and behind, the dog snarled, springing upwards on that first tilt of rock. Above them, the stone face was smooth for nine or ten feet, no holds anywhere, the entrance to a corrie beyond.

There was no choice and Chavasse linked hands into a stirrup. 'Go on, up you go!'

She had sense enough not to argue, but stepped into his hands and was pushed up in one smooth movement that took her over the edge.

The Doberman came after them, scaling the cataract of stone in a series of fantastic bounds, landing no more than a foot below Chavasse, jaws gaping. He kicked out savagely sending it scrambling down. It landed, surefooted as a cat, on a great block of stone below and bounded up again.

Chavasse turned, his back to the rock, and pulled out the Smith & Wesson. The Doberman landed at his side, its paws secured a grip on the ledge and it hung there, its body brushing his leg. It snarled, opened the great jaws to strike and he pushed the Smith & Wesson inside and fired twice.

The back of the animal's head simply dissolved as the heavy magnum bullets smashed through bone and flesh and it spun backwards into space, bouncing from the rocks below, falling clear to the plateau.

Stavrou was halfway across and he paused with a cry of anger, raised his arm and fired a wild shot that ricocheted amongst the rocks to the left. Chavasse fired in reply, sending him running for cover. He stuffed the Smith & Wesson into his pocket and looked up.

Asta peered over the edge, lying on her stomach and extended a hand. He reached up, their fingers locked and he jumped, his right toe finding purchase in a tiny crack. A moment later, he was over the edge and lying beside her.

It was impossible to see the base of the slope, but a rattle of stones told them that Stavrou was climbing. There was no sign of the others.

'We seem to have lost the Munros,' Asta said.

Chavasse shook his head. 'I wouldn't be too sure. They've been born and bred in this country, remember, and they know the mountains. I should say they're already on their way to the top by some other route.'

'And Max?'

'Gone after the ambush party in the Land Rover if he has any sense. We'd better get moving.'

The corrie slanted back up the slope, a great jagged funnel, choked with boulders and scree and they scrambled up, never stopping until they emerged on to a wide ledge.

Above them, the crest of the ridge lifted in a gentle slope and they scrambled over the edge ten minutes later and found themselves on the rim of the main plateau, a grey, silent world of mist and rain.

There was a faint cry carried by the wind from somewhere on the right. Chavasse turned as Hector Munro emerged over the far rim. He paused, raising his shotgun, and then lowered it, realising he was hopelessly out of range and Chavasse urged Asta forward.

They ran across the plateau, picking their way between great jagged boulders, slipping and sliding over the rough ground and as they neared the far side, Rory Munro emerged from broken ground to the right.

Chavasse swung towards him and Munro had no time to take aim, and then they met, breast to breast, the shotgun between them.

Chavasse didn't hesitate. His knee swung up into the unprotected groin. Rory's mouth opened wide in a gasp of agony and he keeled over. Chavasse hurled the shotgun away over the rocks and as he turned, there was an angry cry and Hector Munro ran towards him. Stavrou twenty or thirty yards behind.

Asta waited on the rim of the plateau. Chavasse took her hand and they went over and down into the mist and rain, riding a great apron of shale and loose earth that moved beneath them.

They landed on a bare, steep slope, rough tussocks of grass growing from crevasses, making the descent difficult, slowing them considerably so that it was a good fifteen minutes before they emerged on a hillside above the glen and moved down through the heather.

But their pursuers were not far behind. At one point Chavasse was aware of a faint cry and, turning, saw Stavrou through a gap in the mist, a couple of hundred feet above them.

They plunged down through a plantation of young firs, arms raised to protect their faces from the branches. When they emerged on the other side, Asta staggered and would have fallen if he hadn't caught her.

She leaned against him, struggling for breath. 'Sorry, Paul, but I can't keep this up for much longer.' And then her eyes widened and she pointed down into the valley. 'Is that them?'

A Land Rover was pulled in at the roadside. Not one of Donner's, but unmistakably Army with the unit and divisional crests painted on its bonnet and sides in bright colours. An officer in jeep coat and peaked cap stood beside it, a map in his hands.

Chavasse called out, waving wildly and, miraculously, the officer turned and looked up. Chavasse grabbed Asta's hand and they plunged down the final slope through the heather, sliding into the ditch at the side of the road. They picked themselves up and ran to the car.

The officer looked towards them, a hand above his eyes to shield them from the rain. He leaned down and said something and his driver got out from behind the wheel and joined him.

It was only in the final moment that Chavasse realised that he was too late. That the driver carried a machine-pistol. That the officer was Jack Murdoch.

As he and Asta halted, waiting helplessly, a Land Rover roared out of the mist behind them and skidded to a halt. Max Donner got out and ran forward, his face cold and angry.

'You know, you've been asking for this, sport,' he said and his fist swung, connecting high on the right cheek, sending Chavasse back into the ditch.

Asta turned and ran and further along the road, Stavrou slid down to the road and moved to meet her, As he dragged her back, Hector Munro and Rory appeared from the plantation above.

'Get down here,' Donner called. 'You're going to ruin everything.'

There was a track on the other side of the road and he nodded to Stavrou. 'Drive the Land Rover in there and make it quick. We haven't got much time.' He pulled Chavasse to his feet and produced a Mauser from his pocket, a bulbous silencer on the end of the barrel. 'Into the trees, sport,' he said grimly. 'I had plans for you, but I can always change them.'

Asta ran past him to Chavasse's side and together they moved across the road into the pine trees as Stavrou drove the Land Rover out of sight. The Munros followed looking slightly bewildered.

They all halted beside the Land Rover, screened from the road by trees and Donner turned to face them. 'And now we wait.'

It was quiet with the rain hissing down through the trees and then in the distance, they heard the sound of a vehicle approaching from the south. As the sound drew nearer, Chavasse realised that there was more than one engine—probably two, which seemed reasonable. A troop carrier for the men, a staff car for the officers.

They started to slow and through the green screen of the pine trees he was aware of movement and then the engines stopped altogether and Murdoch's voice was raised, warm and pleasant, eager to please.

'Captain Bailey, sir, with Colonel von Bayern's party?'

'That's right,' a strange voice said. 'What's all this, then?'

'Lieutenant Grant, sir, attached to Movement Control, Mallaig. There's flooding on the road up ahead, sir, due to last night's heavy rain. My C.O. thought I'd better come to meet you with an alternative route in case of trouble.'

'Surely it can't be as bad as all that if you got here?'

'I only just managed to get across the bridge at Craigie,' Murdoch said, 'and the water was three feet deep then and rising fast. I don't think anything else but a Land Rover could have made it.'

'All right then, what about this alternative route you mentioned?'

'We go through the pass into Glenmore, sir. Poor roads I'm afraid and a longer way round, but we've arranged for you to halt for lunch at Glenmore House.'

'Well, that sounds promising at any rate,' Bailey replied. 'You take the lead. We'll follow.'

There was the slam of a door, followed by another, a strange, hollow silence and then the engines coughed into life. As they died into the distance, Donner turned to Chavasse and grinned.

'Simple when you know how, sport.'

CHAPTER THIRTEEN
ENTER VON BAYERN

DONNER STOOD IN FRONT OF THE fireplace in the library, adjusting the collar of his uniform. He fastened the top button, placed the peaked cap at a slight angle on his head and nodded in satisfaction.

Behind him, the door opened and Asta entered, Stavrou behind her. Donner turned with a grin and held his arms wide. 'Will I do?'

Asta's eyes burned with hate. 'If I had a gun, I'd kill you, Max,' she said flatly.

He took off his cap and crossed in two quick strides, holding her shoulders gently. 'Asta, I love you. I've always loved you. Just a few hours and I'll be back and we'll fly away from this place—far away where no one can touch us.'

She shook her head. 'I won't go, Max.'

'Give yourself a chance. You'll come round,' he said confidently.

'You murdered my mother,' she said. 'When you touch me, I want to be sick.'

He took an involuntary step back and there was real horror in his eyes. 'Now look, Asta, you've got it all wrong....'

She didn't give him a chance. 'Ruth told me. It's no use trying to deny it now. And I saw what you did to Fergus. I can believe anything after that.'

His face hardened. 'You don't leave me much choice, do you?' He nodded to Stavrou. 'Put her in the cellars with the rest of them and send Munro in here.'

She turned without a word and went out, Stavrou at her heels. Donner walked across to the desk, picked up the Mauser with the bulbous silencer on the barrel and checked the magazine.

The door opened and Murdoch entered with Boris Souvorin. The Russian wore the uniform of a sergeant-major in the German Army and Murdoch, who was to take Bailey's place, had Intelligence Corps insignia on the shoulders of his battledress tunic.

'We're ready when you are,' he said.

Donner nodded. 'Get the men into the truck. I'll be with you in five minutes.'

They went out quickly and he slipped the Mauser into his hip pocket and lit a cigarette. The door opened and Hector Munro came in followed by Stavrou.

Donner turned to face him. 'We're leaving now. Stavrou is staying, but he has things to do, so I want you and your son to help guard the prisoners in the cellar.'

'Well now, I'm not so sure about that,' the old man said. 'I don't like the way this thing is shaping up and that's a fact.'

'And what do you intend to do about it?' Donner said. 'Go to the authorities?' He shook his head. 'I thought you had brains, Hector. You're already in this up to your neck. No turning back now.'

The old man stood there, indecision on his face and Donner slapped him on the shoulder. 'Five hundred apiece for you and Rory when I get back this evening. After that, you can go where you want.'

Munro's eyes brightened. 'By God, that's money, Mr. Donner. Real money.'

'Get to it then.' Donner said and the old man turned and went out quickly.

Donner put on his cap and picked up his gloves. 'You are leaving now?' Stavrou said in Russian.

'I've one small thing to attend to first,' Donner said. 'Come with me.'

He went out into the hall, mounted the stairs quickly and moved along the landing. When he opened the door to Ruth Murray's room, she was lying on the bed, a glass in her hand.

She put it down and got to her feet. 'Max, darling, I haven't seen you all day.'

When she was close enough, he struck her heavily in the face, knocking her back across the bed. She got to her feet again, dazed, blood on her lip.

'What is it, Max? What have I done?'

'You bitch,' he said savagely. 'You told Asta about her mother—about what happened at Lesbos.'

She looked genuinely bewildered. 'No. Max! No—it isn't possible.'

He picked up the brandy decanter and held it front of her face. 'It was this—don't you realise? You were drunk, as you always are. So damned drunk you didn't know what you were doing.'

He tossed the decanter across the room and shoved her back on to the bed. She was completely sober, her eyes wide with horror. 'I didn't mean it, Max. I didn't mean any harm.'

'You never do, angel.'

'What are you going to do?' she whispered hoarsely.

'Do?' He smiled coldly. 'I'm going to give you to Stavrou.'

She shook her head several times from side to side. 'No, Max, you wouldn't do that.'

'Wouldn't I?' Donner said and he turned and went out, closing the door behind him.

Stavrou stood looking down at her, no expression on the cold, cruel face and then he did something she had never known him do before. He laughed.

As he took his first step towards her, she screamed and staggered to her feet, pushing a chair between them. He kicked it to one side as negligently as one might kick a football and she turned and ran to the French windows, wrenching them open so violently that a pane of glass shattered.

But there was no way out. The balcony led nowhere except to the stone terrace at the front of the house forty feet below. She turned and as Stavrou appeared in the window, gave a heart-rending cry and flung herself over the rail.

The cell into which they pushed Chavasse had a barred grill in the door, but no window and when the door closed behind him he found himself in almost total darkness. There was a rustle on the other side of the room and he was aware of a darker shadow against the wall, the white blur of a face.

'Who's there?' he said sharply.

'Ah, English,' the other said, speaking with a slight accent. 'How interesting. Presumably you are on our side?'

'That depends very much on who you are,' Chavasse said.

'Allow me to introduce myself. Gunther von Bayern, Colonel, Military Intelligence Corps, German Army. You don't mind if I call it that, do you? As far as I'm concerned there *is* only one.'

'Chavasse—Paul Chavasse.'

'Ah, French?'

'And English. You wouldn't have such a thing as a cigarette would you?'

'Be my guest.'

The face that leapt out of the darkness when the match flared was wedge-shaped, the skin drawn tightly over high cheekbones. The eyes were black and flecked with amber and seemed to change colour in the flickering light. He was about forty-five, a handsome, smiling man with a deceptively lazy drawl that didn't fool Chavasse for one minute.

'Wasn't there a Captain Bailey with you?'

Von Bayern nodded. 'Our liaison officer. Poor fellow, when we drove into the courtyard of this damned place and found ourselves under the guns of men who were apparently soldiers in my own army, he tried to make a run for it.'

'They gunned him down?'

'I'm afraid so. Don't you think it's about time you told me what this is all about?'

Chavasse crouched down beside him and started to talk. It took a surprisingly short time and when he finished, von Bayern chuckled softly. 'You know, one really must give credit where it is due. The plan has all the simplicity of genius.'

'And it will work,' Chavasse said. 'It will work and there isn't a damn thing we can do about it.'

Footsteps sounded in the passage outside and when he hurried to the grill, he saw Asta going past with Stavrou. When he called, she turned and hurried across.

'Are you all right, Paul?'

'Fine, angel.'

Von Bayern's face appeared beside him. 'May I have the pleasure of an introduction?'

'Asta Svensson—Gunther von Bayern.'

'Distinctly my pleasure,' von Bayern said, and Stavrou, scowling, dragged her away.

They heard a door slam further down the passage, a key turn in the lock and Stavrou went past on his own.

'A nasty looking piece of work, that one,' von Bayern observed.

'Stavrou?' Chavasse nodded. 'He's supposed to be Greek.'

Von Bayern shook his head. 'Definitely from east of the Urals. I fought too many of his breed in my youth to be mistaken.'

He offered Chavasse another cigarette and they sat down on an old wooden packing case. 'A charming girl, by the way. Are you in love with her?'

'You don't pull your punches, do you?'

'My dear Paul—you don't mind if I call you that, do you? There really isn't time for any other approach. Life is always cruel, usually unjust and often very wonderful in between. It pays to recognise those moments.'

'You're a strange one,' Chavasse said. 'Here we are, condemned to rot in this dump for an unspecified period while the world crumbles around us and you philosophise. What does it take to depress you?'

Von Bayern chuckled. 'I was in Stalingrad—in fact I am one of the few men I know who actually got out of Stalingrad. Everything else in my life has been a distinct improvement. It would be impossible for it to be anything else.'

There was a sudden rattle at the door and when Chavasse turned, Hector Munro leered in at them through the grill. 'Well, well, now, isn't that nice?' he said. 'Is it warm enough for you, Mr. Chavasse?'

Chavasse moved across to the door and looked out at him. 'Where's Donner? I'd like to speak to him.'

'He left better than an hour ago,' Hector Munro chuckled. 'You're in my care now, my brave wee mannie. Now I am going to eat my fill of Mr. Donner's good food and drink my fill of Mr. Donner's fine whisky. Maybe in a couple of hours or perhaps three I'll be back to see if you've frozen to death.'

His laughter echoed back to them as he went up the steps and the door at the top shut with harsh finality.

Donner stood in the wheelhouse of the LCT and looked through a porthole at the length of the ship. The hold was a steel shell and the Bedford troop carrier and the olive green staff car belonging to their party seemed to be the only cargo. Beyond were the great steel bow doors of the beaching exit.

The sea was choppy with a slight breeze from the north-west and although the mist and the rain had reduced visibility, they had made good time from Mallaig.

The captain, a second lieutenant in the Royal Corps of Transport, a fair-haired young man in a heavy white polo sweater, came in from the bridge and gave the helmsman an order.

'Port five.'

'Port five of wheel on, sir.'

'Steady now.'

'Steady. Steering two-o-three, sir.'

Donner opened his silver case and turned to Murdoch. 'Cigarette, Captain Bailey?'

'Thank you, sir.'

The young lieutenant turned. 'Not long now, sir. About another twenty minutes.'

Donner moved to the porthole and looked out. In the middle distance and looking surprisingly large, he saw the islands; Barra, Sandray and Fhada to the south.

'Perhaps I'll have the chance to offer you a drink when we land, lieutenant,' he said.

The young man shook his head. 'I'm awfully sorry, sir. I'm only stopping here for long enough to put you and your party ashore, then I proceed to Lewis. I'm carrying electronic equipment they've been waiting rather impatiently for at Guided Weapons H.Q.'

Donner nodded. 'I understand. Duty, after all, must come before everything else.'

His accent was just right and he went out on to the bridge, wrapping the oilskin coat they had loaned him about his shoulders. Not long now and as Fhada moved closer out of the mist, he stayed there watching it, so still that he might have been carved out of stone.

The harbour was not very large and the landing craft beached beside an old stone jetty. One or two small sailing dinghies were pulled up on the sand above high water mark, but the only sizable craft were an old thirty-foot lobster boat and a beautiful power boat—a twenty-five footer, painted white and green.

When the bow doors opened, the staff car went out first, driving across a specially constructed concrete apron to the start of a tarmacadam road. A Land Rover was parked there and as the staff car approached, a tall, greying, middle-aged man in heavy jeep coat and black beret got out.

The staff car braked to a halt and Donner went to meet him. 'Von Bayern,' he said, holding out his hand.

'Major Charles Endicott.' The other saluted briefly then shook hands. 'I wonder whether you'd like to drive up to the mess in my Land Rover?'

'A pleasure.'

Donner climbed into the passenger seat and Endicott took the wheel. He grinned as he pushed the starter and drove away. 'Strictly against regulations this, but we're pretty easy-going out here.'

Behind them, the troop carrier was already moving across the beach and Donner turned to see the bow doors of the LCT close. A moment later, it was reversing into the harbour.

'They don't waste much time, do they?' he said.

Endicott shook his head. 'They're good lads.'

Donner nodded and lit a cigarette. 'A beautiful boat there in the harbour. She is yours, I understand?'

Endicott smiled. 'The pride of my life. Built by Akerboon, steel hull, twin screws. She'll do twenty-five knots any day of the week.'

'Ah, an enthusiast.'

'Something like that.'

They topped the hill above the harbour and emerged on to the great sloping plateau that was the western half of the island. Donner could see the station at once, a scattering of flat-roofed concrete huts built to withstand the fury of the storms that swept in across this small island too frequently for comfort. Beyond them, a row of ugly concrete mounds faced the Atlantic.

'The missile pens,' Endicott said. 'As you can imagine, this place makes an ideal range, but because of the extremes of weather, we're compelled to site the weapons themselves underground.'

'You have been having some real success with Firebird, I hear?'

Endicott grinned. 'Even the Americans are going to have to sit up and take notice of that little baby.'

As the staff car slowed behind them, he released the brake and drove on across the barren landscape towards the scattered buildings.

'I'm afraid we don't have a great deal to offer in the way of comfort,' he said as he drew up outside the officers' mess, 'but I've seen worse.'

The staff car pulled up alongside and as they went up the steps into the mess, Murdoch joined them. It was pleasant enough inside, like similar places the world over. A scattering of armchairs, magazines on the tables, the Queen's portrait behind the bar.

'Whisky suit you, Colonel?' Endicott asked, and when Donner nodded, turned to the barman. 'The rest of my staff will be along in a moment. Only five officers here, of course. We've a very small establishment.'

Donner accepted the whisky, moved to the window and looked out to where his men were dismounting from the troop carrier, each with a canvas military hold-all in his hand. A young Battery Sergeant-Major was talking to Souvorin as the senior German N.C.O., obviously telling him where they were to be quartered.

Donner turned. 'I'd like my men to hang on for a few minutes if you don't mind, Major. I want a word with them before they disperse.'

'Certainly, Colonel,' Endicott replied and at that moment his officers started to arrive.

There were three subalterns, a full lieutenant and Endicott's second in command, a Captain Harrison. Donner was introduced to each in turn and the younger officers particularly were obviously rather nervous.

'When do we start work, Major?' Donner asked when they were all on their second drink.

'Oh, I thought the day after tomorrow, Colonel,' Endicott said. 'That should give your men plenty of time to get acclimatised.'

Donner moved to the window and nodded to Souvorin. Two of his men walked up the steps, entered the mess and closed the door behind them.

'No, I'm afraid the day after tomorrow will be far too late, Major,' Donner said.

The two men at the door unzipped their holdalls and produced machine pistols. There was a moment of stunned silence and Endicott put down his glass and moved forward.

'Look here, what in the hell is this?'

'We are taking over, Major Endicott,' Donner said. 'And if you know what's good for you, you'll co-operate.'

'You must be mad,' Endicott said angrily and he turned towards the bar. 'Jackson—ring through to the Orderly Room.'

Donner took the Mauser from his pocket, cocked it and shot Endicott through the back of his head at short range, killing him instantly, blood and brains spattering across the floor as he fell.

The obscenity of his death was somehow intensified by the almost complete lack of sound from the silenced Mauser and one of the young subalterns turned away and was sick on the spot.

'Captain Harrison,' Donner said calmly to the second-in-command. 'We're going to dismantle Firebird and you are going to help us do it.'

'I'll see you in hell first,' Harrison said.

Donner shook his head. 'Oh no you won't because if you don't co-operate, I'll parade this unit and give every fifth man what I've just given Endicott.'

He meant it and Harrison knew it. He sagged down into a chair and Donner turned to Murdoch. 'All right. Take over the camp and don't forget to make sure of the wireless room first.'

Murdoch went outside, the door banging behind him. Donner turned and lit a cigarette. He looked down at Harrison for a moment, grinned and patted him on the shoulder.

'Cheer up, sport,' he said in his normal voice. 'You could be like Endicott. You could be dead.'

CHAPTER FOURTEEN

Crash-Out

'DID YOU KNOW,' VON BAYERN SAID, 'that last year in Munich, there were at least half a dozen cases of injuries to the eye caused by champagne corks? What a city. Really, Paul, there is nowhere quite like it.'

'It certainly sounds quite a place,' Chavasse said.

'What a time I could show you. Soon it will be the *Oktoberfest*. Parties, balls—the most beautiful women in Germany. Good food, fine wine.' He sighed heavily. 'How long have we been here?'

Chavasse checked his watch. 'About four hours. They'll be on Fhada by now. I'd give a lot to know what's happening.'

'From what you tell me of Donner I should say things are probably going very much according to plan.'

'One thing I don't understand is how Donner intends to get back here from Fhada.'

'You are sure he will come?'

Chavasse nodded. 'He wouldn't leave Asta, He's obsessed by her. His one weakness, I suppose. He said he'd be taking me along and a session in the Lubianka is something I can definitely do without.'

'And how does he intend to leave here?'

'He has his own plane parked in the meadow on the other side of the house—a Beaver.'

'Interesting,' von Bayern said. 'He's certainly thought of everything.'

'And not a damned thing we can do about it. Even if we got out of here, reached Mallaig and they put a general alert into operation, by the time they reached Fhada it would very probably be too late and, as far as I know, it's impossible to land by air.'

'That's not quite true,' von Bayern said. 'I was very thoroughly briefed on the island before coming and there was considerable information on flying conditions which interested me particularly as an old pilot.'

'I didn't realise you'd been a flyer.'

'Oh, yes—I was in the Brandenberg Division for a considerable part of the war—special operations. Handling a plane was just part of the job. Apparently there is a real problem in the Hebrides with down-draughts which makes the use of helicopters often impractical. So many crashed attempting to put down on Fhada, that last year your Army Air Corps experimented in landing light aircraft at the northern end of the island.'

'But I thought the cliffs were about six hundred feet high?'

'True, but when the tide goes out, it uncovers a very large area of firm sand. They found that landing was no trouble. Unfortunately, the tide turns so quickly that it was impossible for the planes to stay very long and there were other problems. The carriage of cargo up the cliffs and so on. I understand the idea has been abandoned.'

Chavasse turned to look at him, his face pale in the half light. 'Could you fly a Beaver by any chance?'

'But of course.' Von Bayern shrugged. 'A common enough military aircraft.'

Chavasse got to his feet and walked restlessly to the other end of the cell. 'Fifteen minutes' flying time from here to Fhada, it couldn't take more.'

'And we could all go,' von Bayern said. 'My men included. A nasty surprise for Herr Donner. Unfortunate that we can't get out of here, isn't it?'

Chavasse kicked the door in impotent rage and the German pulled him down beside him. 'Have another cigarette, Paul, and relax. Anger is a negative emotion. We must wait patiently and grasp what opportunities present themselves. There is nothing else to be done.'

It was perhaps half an hour later, that they became aware of voices raised in song, faint in the distance and then the door at the top of the cellar stairs was opened and heavy steps descended.

The singing stopped and Hector Munro appeared at the grill, Rory at his shoulder. They laughed foolishly, obviously half drunk and Hector kicked the door.

'Are ye still there, Mr. Chavasse?'

'I'm here,' Chavasse said. 'What do you want?'

'Just checking,' the old man said. 'I'm in charge here now, you know. Stavrou's away to Loch Dubh to see to things at the castle.' He laughed harshly. 'Are ye comfortable enough in there, the two of you?'

'It could be worse,' Chavasse said. 'It could be a prison cell with a fifteen-year sentence for treason stretching into the distance.' He laughed coldly. 'But why bother? You'll know all about that soon enough.'

The foolish smile disappeared from Rory's face and he turned to his father. 'What's he talking about, Da?'

'Never you heed him,' old Hector said. 'Come this evening, Mr. Donner will be back here to pay us our thousand pounds and we'll be away out of this and damn all this fella will be able to do about it.'

Rory's face cleared. 'Right you are, Da. We'll pick up Fergus at Tomintoul. If we get the evening train from Fort William, we could be in Glasgow in time to catch the nine o'clock boat to Belfast. No passports needed.'

The old man cackled. 'And crossing the border into Eire is no trick for the likes of us.'

What was it von Bayern had said? *You grasped the opportunity that presented itself?* Chavasse gripped the bars of the grill as they started to turn away.

'Just a minute, Munro.' The old man turned, swaying slightly. 'You said something about Fergus waiting for you in Tomintoul?'

'So what?'

Chavasse shook his head and said softly, 'He won't be there, Hector. Donner got to him first.'

The old man stood there staring stupidly at him, his face drained of all colour. 'It's a lie,' he said hoarsely. 'You're lying.'

'Let me out of here and I'll show you.'

'Maybe it's a trick, Da,' Rory Munro said.

'If it is, I'll kill him.' The old man took a bunch of keys from his pocket, tossed them across to his son and thumbed back the hammers of his shotgun. 'Let him out.'

'Do you know what you're doing?' von Bayern whispered.

Chavasse nodded. 'Don't try to be a hero when he opens the door. I don't think it's going to be necessary.'

When he stepped into the corridor, Rory slammed the door shut behind him immediately, locking it again. They both stood there covering him with their shotguns and Chavasse nodded.

'This way,' he said and moved down the passage.

He turned the corner at the end and found the cell he had previously been imprisoned in with no difficulty, recognising it at once by the bar across the door. It was in the next cell that Asta had told him she found Fergus.

'He's in there,' Chavasse said.

Hector glanced at him suspiciously, then nodded to Rory. 'Watch him. I'll take a look.'

He opened the door and fumbled for the light switch. A second later, he gave a terrible cry and his shotgun clattered to the floor. Rory turned involuntary to glance inside and his eyes widened with horror.

'Help me!' the old man moaned. 'Help me get him down.'

Rory leaned his gun against the wall and ran inside. Chavasse moved into the doorway and watched as they lifted the pathetic broken body from the hook and lowered it. The old man dropped to his knees and gently touched the blood-streaked face. When he looked up, there were tears in his eyes.

'Donner did this?'

Chavasse nodded. 'Miss Svensson was a witness.'

'Hung up and butchered like a side of beef. I was bought and paid for, so murdering my son didn't matter.' His hand came out of his pocket holding the bunch of keys and he tossed them across. 'You'll be needing these, I'm thinking.'

Chavasse picked up the old man's shotgun and collected Rory's on the way out and neither of them made the slightest objection, trapped in a world of their own private grief.

He ran back along the passage, calling Asta's name as he went and she answered him at once. There were at least a dozen keys on the ring, but they included a master key obviously intended for all the doors and in a moment she was in his arms.

'What happened?'

'The Munros have just changed sides. I showed them Fergus.'

They hurried along to his own cell and von Bayern stared through the grill in astonishment as Chavasse unlocked the door.

'A miracle, my friend?'

'Something like that. I'll explain later.' As the German emerged, Chavasse gave him one of the shotguns and turned to Asta. 'Is there a gun room upstairs?'

She nodded. 'Next to the library.'

Chavasse handed the keys to von Bayern. 'I'll see what I can dig up. You release the others and we'll meet in the hall.'

He went up the cellar steps, Asta at his heels and from below, they could hear the excited babble of voices as von Bayern moved to release his nine soldiers and the two British Army drivers.

It was quiet in the passage outside the kitchen and Asta led the way quickly through to the hall. When they went into the library, a fire still burned fitfully on the hearth and she opened the far door into the gun room.

Such rooms were a common feature of old Scottish houses with estates which provided good shooting, but remembering Duncan Craig's remarks about Donner's lack of interest in hunting Chavasse didn't expect to find a great deal.

It could have been worse. Although most of the racks were empty, there were three double-barrelled shotguns, a Winchester .22 target rifle, probably kept for the rooks and an old .45 Ballard & Moore, powerful enough to stop an elephant.

Unfortunately there was only ammunition for the Winchester and the shotguns and regretfully he left the Ballard & Moore and went back through the library.

When they went into the hall, von Bayern was already there, his men standing at attention before him in a straight line, the two British soldiers on the end. He turned quickly and Chavasse handed him the three shotguns and the Winchester.

'Best I could do, I'm afraid. Have you told them what's happening?'

'As much as there was time for.'

Chavasse glanced down the line of soldiers. They looked tough and fit, but rather more intelligent than the average infantry soldier and he noticed that two of them wore glasses.

'These boys are really technicians, aren't they?' he said. 'Electronics experts.'

'And good soldiers, too. Have no fear, my friend. They know what they're getting in to.' He nodded to the senior N.C.O., a fair-haired, handsome man in his middle thirties. 'Sergeant-Major Steiner here served for five years in the French Foreign Legion Paratroops. He was at Dien-Bien-Phu.' He grinned and tossed the Winchester to Steiner who caught it expertly. 'Friend Donner may get a shock.'

One of the RASC drivers was a corporal and Chavasse moved across to him, 'What's your name, Corporal?'

'Jackson, sir, and this is Driver Benson. I don't know who you are, sir, but we're just as keen to have a go as the Jerries.'

'I'm sorry,' Chavasse said. 'But one of you will have to stay to take the Land Rover into Mallaig to notify H.Q. of what's happening.' He turned to Asta. 'You can go, too, Asta. You'll be able to tell them everything they need to know.'

She nodded, her face pale. 'What about Ruth?'

'She doesn't seem to be around so she must have gone down to Loch Dubh with Stavrou. Just forget about her. No one can help her now.'

Corporal Jackson tossed a coin, catching it neatly as Benson called. He extended his palm. Benson looked at the coin and his face dropped.

'All right, sir. I'll take the young lady into Mallaig.'

Already von Bayern and his men were moving out and Chavasse turned to Asta and groped for her hand. She looked up at him, her eyes shadowed.

'Take care, Paul.'

'Don't I always?' he said and went after the others.

There was silence in the hall when he had gone and she stood there looking suddenly very young. Benson coughed and cleared his throat. 'We'd better get going, miss.'

'Just give me a moment,' she said. 'I'd like to see them leave.'

She moved to the window and watched the small knot of men running across the meadow beyond the poplar trees to where the Beaver squatted at the far end. It was an excellent take-off, she'd had enough experience of flying to be able to tell that and the plane banked in a great sweeping curve to the right when it was no more than two or three hundred feet in the air, and turned out to sea.

'All right now, miss?' Benson said.

She nodded slowly and they crossed the hall and went out into the courtyard at the rear of the house. The Land Rover in the garage was the one Murdoch had driven earlier that morning and still carried the fake insignia which had been used to fool von Bayern's party. Obviously Stavrou had driven to the loch in the other one.

She climbed into the passenger seat and Benson got behind the wheel. The starter rattled hollowly when he pressed it, but the engine refused to turn over. He tried the choke with no better success and cursed.

'Sounds as if the damned thing's been immobilised, miss. I'd better take a look.'

He walked round to the front of the vehicle and Stavrou appeared in the garage entrance, a machine pistol in his hands. Asta cried a warning. Benson swung round, alarm on his face and Stavrou drove him back against the bonnet of the Land Rover with a quick burst.

The savage hammering seemed to fill the building, bouncing back from the walls and as Benson spun crazily and fell to the floor, Asta saw Hector and Rory Munro emerge from the back door of the house on the other side of the courtyard.

Stavrou fired, a line of bullets cutting across the wall of the house as he swung, smashing a window, catching Rory Munro as he jumped for the shelter of the door after his father.

Stavrou turned, his face terrible in its calmness and Asta reached for the Land Rover's heavy steel starting handle, scrambled out and backed away from him. He placed the machine pistol carefully on the bonnet of the vehicle and moved towards her.

She threw the starting handle at him with all her strength and, as he ducked, ran for the other side of the Land Rover. He caught her by one arm, moving with amazing speed for such a big man, swinging her hard against the wall and struck her back-handed across the jaw, knocking her unconscious.

CHAPTER FIFTEEN

FORCE OF ARMS

SITTING IN THE COCKPIT OF THE Beaver beside von Bayern, a chart on his knees, Chavasse saw Fhada lift out of the sea on the horizon, a grey hump under cumulous clouds, the great six hundred foot cliffs at the northern end wreathed in mist.

They were flying at no more than two hundred feet above the sea, the German's hands steady on the wheel. Rain rattled against the windows and, below, the grey-green surface of the sea was whipped into white-caps.

'If we come in from the north, the cliffs should conceal our approach,' von Bayern said.

'What about the wind direction? Will it be okay for landing?'

'Good enough. It's the down-draughts from those cliffs we'll have to watch for.'

He turned to starboard a couple of points, running north-west into the Atlantic and when the cliffs of Fhada were to port, altered course again, dropping towards the sea, making his approach at no more than a hundred feet.

The great black cliffs, streaked with guano, reared above them and, below, Chavasse saw a shining expanse of wet sand a quarter of a mile wide.

Von Bayern took the Beaver in on a dummy run, feeling for the wind and a cross current from the island caught them so that they rocked violently. He swung the wheel full circle, taking the Beaver out to sea again, banked, and came in low over the waves, throttling back and dropping his flaps.

The wheels seemed to touch the surface of the water and then they were down, biting into the hard wet sand and the jagged rocks at the base of the cliffs rushed towards them. To Chavasse, it seemed as if they might never stop and then, suddenly, the Beaver was turning to port, completely under control.

After the engine was switched off, the propeller spun for a moment or two and then stopped. Von Bayern turned and smiled through the silence. 'A nice plane. He certainly keeps her in good trim, I'll say that for him.'

'I'm beginning to wonder how we won the war,' Chavasse said and he turned and followed Sergeant-Major Steiner through the cabin door.

The coldness hit him at once and the light rain blowing in from the Atlantic carried the sharp promise of winter with it.

The Germans stood together in a group talking in low voices. Chavasse noticed that Corporal Jackson was joining in and called him over. 'You know some German, then, Corporal?'

Jackson grinned. 'Should do, sir. I've spent enough time in B.A.O.R. My wife, Hilda—she's from Dortmund.'

'Good show,' Chavasse said. 'That's what we're going to speak from now on.' He turned to the rest of the party as von Bayern got out of the plane and said in German, 'This is a military operation, so far as I'm concerned, Colonel von Bayern is in command.'

'Thank you, Paul.' Von Bayern smiled briefly and addressed the men. 'Always supposing that our arrival hasn't been spotted, we have one advantage—complete surprise, plus the fact that you are all familiar with the terrain of the island and layout of the camp, from your two-week period of instruction and briefing in Germany before leaving. Speed is essential, so I don't propose to waste any more time in talk. Our first objective is the armoury. How we get inside is something I shall decide when we get there.'

He nodded to Chavasse and they turned and led the way along the base of the cliffs. From the sea, they had resembled an impregnable stone wall, but a closer inspection revealed great gullies and fissures providing an easy, if strenuous route up from the beach.

Chavasse scrambled over the top fifteen minutes later into a nightmare world of broken grey boulders, sparse grass and clinging mist. Von Bayern followed and they waited for the others to join them.

'From here, the ground slopes steeply to the camp at the other end of the island,' von Bayern said. 'The mist will conceal us for most of the way. After that, we stick to the broken ground.'

'How far?' Chavasse asked him.

'A little over a quarter of a mile.'

They set off down the hillside, keeping together, Chavasse and von Bayern in the lead, moving into a strange and alien world, the grey, damp walls of mist, pressing in on them.

As the ground fell away beneath them, they moved faster and as they descended, visibility increased until finally, the mist disappeared altogether.

A dry stream bed gave them the cover they needed and they followed it for several hundred yards until von Bayern finally called a halt. He and Chavasse crawled up the bank and peered over the edge.

The camp was spread before them no more than a hundred and fifty yards away and von Bayern beckoned to Steiner to join them. As they watched, a truck pulling a trailer carrying a small rocket emerged from behind the missile pens. It drove through the camp and took the road down towards the harbour.

'Firebird?' Chavasse said.

'One would imagine so. The officers' mess is the building directly behind the flagstaff. The armoury is beyond. The radio room is in the concrete tower.'

Sergeant-Major Steiner pointed to a long, low concrete building to their right. 'Isn't that the fuel store, Colonel?'

'That's right.'

'I wonder why they've put a guard on it?'

As he pointed, they saw one of Donner's men step out of the entrance, a machine pistol slung from his shoulders.

'A good place to imprison thirty-eight men, from the look of it,' Chavasse said.

Von Bayern nodded. 'You're probably right. The interesting thing is that the trawler Donner mentioned isn't in the harbour, so presumably they're still waiting for her.'

'That makes sense,' Chavasse said. 'Especially if that *was* Firebird we just saw going down to the harbour. That trawler isn't going to come in until she's sure they're absolutely ready for her. I bet they've got the whole thing timed to such a degree that she's in and out again in half an hour.'

'It would be a pity to frighten her away,' von Bayern said. 'And the moment we start shooting, whoever is in that radio room will do just that.'

'All right,' Chavasse said. 'Give me one good man to help me and I'll tackle the radio room. Donner's only got thirteen men including himself, so he can't have more than two or three up there. We might be able to jump them before any shooting starts.'

'A good idea. I'll give you Steiner. I have a feeling you're going to need him. I'll leave two men here to tackle the guard on that fuel store and move in on the armoury with the rest in exactly fifteen minutes. You'd better take a shotgun each, by the way. Whatever happens in that tower is going to be very much at close quarters.'

Chavasse nodded. 'I hope to God you get into that armoury. If you don't, we won't last long against automatic weapons.'

'The thought had occurred to me.' Von Bayern grinned. 'Do your best to survive, Paul. You promised to sample the delights of the *Oktoberfest* with me in Munich at the end of the month, remember.'

'It had better be worth the blood and sweat, that's all,' Chavasse said and he moved away along the stream bed with Steiner.

It petered out a hundred yards further on and they crawled across broken ground to the shelter of the missile pens. From there, they skirted the back of a Nissen hut and paused in its shelter, no more than ten yards from the concrete tower. It was perhaps fifty feet high and obviously contained a spiral staircase, narrow slotted windows going up at ten-foot intervals.

The radio room was at the very top, a narrow balcony encircling its glass walls and a steel emergency ladder ran from top to bottom of the building.

Chavasse pointed to the ladder. 'That's my way to the top, Sergeant-Major. You take it from inside.'

Steiner grinned, showing even white teeth. 'Rather you than me. I never did have much of a head for heights.'

Chavasse moved forward quickly and holding the shotgun in one hand, started to climb. Steiner waited until he was ten or fifteen feet high and then he ran forward, opened the door in the base of the tower and went inside.

A spiral staircase started on his right and there was a door to the left. He started towards the staircase and at the same moment, the door opened and one of Donner's men emerged. He carried a machine pistol in one hand and his reflexes were excellent.

In one quick moment he took in Steiner, the uniform, the fact that he was a stranger. The machine pistol swung up, and Steiner couldn't get close enough to do anything else except give him both barrels full in the face.

As Steiner dropped his shotgun and picked up the machine pistol, heavy steps thundered on the spiral staircase above. He swung round and as a bullet chipped the concrete beside the door, fired a quick burst in reply. There was no sign of his assailant, only the sound of someone going back up the steel stairs. Steiner sat down, pulled off his boots and went after him, silent on stockinged feet.

Chavasse was no more than half way up the ladder when he heard the shooting from inside the tower. He paused, hanging on with one hand, thumbing back the hammers of the shotgun awkwardly with the other and glanced over his shoulder.

The guard outside the armoury was looking up towards him. He took a step forward, unslinging his machine pistol and von Bayern came round the corner, a shotgun in his hands. He drove the butt hard against the unprotected skull, catching the man's machine pistol as he fell.

There was a sudden cry from beyond the officers' mess and three of Donner's men ran towards him. Von Bayern dropped to one knee and drove them back with a long burst and behind him his men crowded into the armoury.

Above Chavasse, a man leaned over the rail and fired at von Bayern, the bullets landing so close that they kicked dirt into the German's face. Chavasse swung the shotgun up, one-handed, firing both barrels at once, the weapon flying from his hand with the shock of the explosion. The man screamed, his face dissolving into a mask of blood and he disappeared. Chavasse lost his footing, hung crazily for a moment, then got a grip with the other hand and started to climb.

When he reached the balcony, he peered over the edge cautiously, but there was no one there except the dead man who lay against the wall, face down. The radio room itself was empty, the door swinging to and fro in the wind and when he went inside, he found, to his relief, that the equipment was still intact.

There was a quick step behind him, a sudden intake of breath and when he turned, Jack Murdoch stood in the doorway, blood on his face where a flying chip of concrete had sliced across the cheek.

'Chavasse!' he said incredulously, and for a moment the revolver in his hand wavered.

Behind him, Steiner emerged from the stairway, silent in stockinged feet. He touched Murdoch once very gently in the back of the neck with the barrel of the machine pistol, reached over and plucked the revolver from his hand.

'You lose, Murdoch.' Chavasse grinned. 'At a conservative estimate, I'd say you'll have about twenty years to sit back and decide where you went wrong. Where's Donner?'

Murdoch laughed unsteadily. 'Well out of this bloody lot. He would be.'

'You mean he isn't here?'

Murdoch nodded. 'He left two hours or more ago. It was all in the plan. Once we'd taken over and things were running smoothly, there was no reason for him to stay.'

'How did he leave?'

'Major Edicott, the C.O. here, had a power boat, Donner found that out months ago. He's on his way back to the mainland now. There's an old pier on the coast about half a mile from Glenmore House. He's supposed to pick up you and Stavrou and the girl and fly out in the Beaver to a landing strip in northern Sweden. From there he re-fuels and flies on to Russia.'

Chavasse laughed harshly. 'That's what he thinks.'

He turned to the rail and, below, von Bayern and his men, armed with automatic rifles from the armoury, swept on across the square, four of Donner's men retreating before them, firing furiously.

Beyond them, the guard at the fuel store had already been overpowered and as Chavasse watched, several officers and a stream of British soldiers emerged and ran forward, spreading out as they came.

Within a few moments it was all over. As two of Donner's men fell, the others threw down their weapons and raised their hands. As Chavasse watched, von Bayern and the British officers came together. There was a brief conversation and then three of the officers and a mixed group of German and British soldiers broke away and hurried down towards the harbour.

Von Bayern looked up and waved. Chavasse waved back and the German and the British officer he had been talking to walked across to the tower with a couple of men.

Chavasse turned to Steiner. 'Got a cigarette?'

Steiner produced a packet from his tunic pocket. Chavasse took one and accepted a light from the old gun-metal petrol lighter the German held out.

The smoke bit deep into his lungs when he inhaled, harsh and satisfying and suddenly he was tired. A moment later, von Bayern arrived with the British officer.

'This is Captain Harrison, Paul. Unfortunately Major Endicott, the commanding officer, was killed before we arrived.'

Harrison shook hands. 'I don't think I've ever been quite so pleased to see anyone in my life before,' he said. 'If you'll excuse me for a moment, I just want to get in touch with Mallaig.'

He went into the radio room, his two men with him and von Bayern turned to Chavasse. 'You are all right? That was a bad moment when I was fired on from the tower. Thank you.'

'One snag,' Chavasse said. 'Donner cleared out a couple of hours ago in the C.O.'s power boat, apparently all according to plan. Remember I said I couldn't understand how he was to get back.'

Von Bayern shrugged. 'I can't see that it will do him any good. With no plane to fly out in, he can't get very far.'

'That's true.'

Harrison came back to join them. 'I've been in touch with Mallaig and they've put out a general alert, admittedly rather belatedly.'

Chavasse frowned and glanced at von Bayern. 'I should have thought they would have heard from Asta and Benson by now.'

'I'm afraid I don't understand,' Harrison said.

Chavasse explained quickly and Harrison returned to the radio room. He was back within two or three minutes, shaking his head. 'No, there's definitely been no sign of Miss Svensson or Driver Benson.'

'We understand Donner left in Major Endicott's power boat some time ago,' von Bayern said. 'Is it a fast craft?'

Harrison nodded. 'Twin screws—Penta petrol engine. Good for twenty-five or thirty knots in the right weather.'

'Is there any other boat in the harbour?'

'Only an old lobster boat. Not a hope of catching him if that's what you're thinking of. I don't think it could make better than five knots.'

Chavasse turned away, his face grim and von Bayern said, 'No boat on earth could catch him now, Paul.'

'And what if something went wrong?' Chavasse demanded. 'What if Asta's still at Glenmore. Donner must almost be there by now.'

'There's always the plane.'

Chavasse turned from the rail eagerly. 'Do you think it's possible?'

'I don't know,' von Bayern shrugged. 'It depends how far the tide has turned. We certainly couldn't manage the party we brought in. You and me and perhaps Steiner—no more.'

'I could let you have a Land Rover,' Harrison said. 'It would have you on top of the cliffs in five minutes from here. They're marvellous vehicles in rough country.'

'Good, then there is no time to waste, Paul,' von Bayern said and he nodded to Steiner who followed him down the stairs.

Harrison took a revolver from his pocket and handed it to Chavasse. 'I picked this up on the way. You'd better have it.'

Chavasse weighed it in his hand and nodded to Murdoch who had been standing at the rail, a silent observer of everything which had taken place.

'One good turn deserves another. There's still the question of the right signal to bring a certain trawler in here to pick up Firebird. I've a feeling our friend here could be very co-operative in that direction if you approached him in the right way.'

Harrison grinned, turning towards Murdoch and Chavasse went down the spiral staircase quickly after the others.

The sergeant who drove them to the top of the cliffs was a keen amateur naturalist and spent most of his spare time on the cliffs and the seashore.

He shook his head briefly in answer to von Bayern's query about the tide. 'It'll be well in now, sir,' he said. 'They go out slow and swing back sudden, if you follow me. Damned treacherous. I've nearly been caught in the rocks down there a time or two, I can tell you.'

The mist had disappeared when they went over the crest of the final hill and braked to a halt and when they moved to the edge of the cliffs, the Beaver was clearly visible close to the rocks below, strangely alien in such a place.

'See what I mean, sir?'

The sergeant pointed and Chavasse looked to where the sea rolled in across the sand in great, hungry breakers. Already at least half of the area on which they had landed was eaten away and the rest was broken up by great trailing fingers of salt water.

'What do you think?' Chavasse said, turning to von Bayern.

The German shrugged. 'Ask me again when I'm sitting at the controls. Come on. We're wasting time.'

They dropped into the nearest gully and went sliding down in a shower of broken stones and earth and the Artillery sergeant went with them.

Chavasse plunged down the final slope of scree and emerged on to the open beach, aware at once of the strong, fresh breeze that blew in directly from the sea.

'One thing in our favour,' von Bayern said, and they ran towards the Beaver.

When they reached it, von Bayern climbed straight inside, followed by Steiner, but the Artillery sergeant grabbed Chavasse by the sleeve. 'It isn't possible, sir,' he said and his face was white. 'You haven't got a clear run. It's all broken up by water channels.'

Chavasse had no time to reply, because the engine coughed into life with a shattering roar, drowning every other sound. He pushed the sergeant away, clambered up into the cabin and Steiner secured the door.

Chavasse went into the cockpit and sat in the co-pilot's seat. 'What do you think?' he yelled above the roar of the engine.

Von Bayern didn't even bother to reply. There was a strange, set smile on his face. He taxied into the wind and gave her full throttle. The Beaver shuddered and seemed to jump forward on a diagonal course to the sea that gave them the longest strip of beach there was left.

They went across one water channel and then another and another, spray flying up in great clouds on either side, von Bayern stamping hard on the rudder bar to keep her straight. And then she lifted, one wing dipping slightly and the breakers were beneath them, the wheels skimming the whitecaps.

But they weren't rising, that was the terrible thing—the nose was dropping and von Bayern didn't seem to be doing anything about it. Quite suddenly, they were moving very fast indeed, the engine note deepening into a full-throated roar and only then did he pull back the control column.

They lifted into the evening sky, climbing fast and behind them on the beach, the Artillery sergeant watched them go, awe on his face.

CHAPTER SIXTEEN

LAST LAP

COMING IN LOW OVER THE COAST, von Bayern tapped Chavasse on the shoulder and pointed down to the old stone jetty below, the power boat moored beside it. There was no need for words. Chavasse took out the revolver Harrison had given him, emptied it and replaced the cartridges one by one.

The land beneath them seemed very green after the rain and, beyond, the sun dropped down towards the mountains and the valleys were filled with purple shadow. They went over a rise and dipped into Glenmore and there was the house beside the stream, the improvised airstrip flanked by poplar trees, the windsock lifting slightly in the breeze on the flagstaff at one end.

It all looked exactly the same when they had left it and for a wild moment Chavasse had a strange feeling that nothing had happened in between at all—that time was a circle turning endlessly on itself, getting nowhere, and then von Bayern turned the Beaver into the wind and dropped her down.

He taxied all the way to the poplar trees before cutting the engine and when the propeller had stopped turning, the silence seemed unnatural.

Von Bayern turned with a slight smile. 'Last lap, Paul.'

Chavasse nodded. 'Are you armed?'

Von Bayern's eyebrows went up and he chuckled. 'My God, I was forgetting. I used a rifle back there on Fhada.'

Steiner, who still carried his machine pistol, produced the revolver he had taken from Murdoch on the tower and passed it over.

'If the colonel will permit me?'

'My pleasure.' Von Bayern hefted the revolver in his hands. 'No sense in taking unnecessary risks at this stage. Work your way round the house and come in from the courtyard, Steiner. Mr. Chavasse and I will take this side.'

Steiner was first out through the cabin door and they watched him move along the line of poplar trees and disappear.

'A good man,' Chavasse said.

Von Bayern nodded. 'The best.'

He led the way to the low wall beyond the poplar trees and they looked across to the terrace at the rear of the house. It was still and quiet, the windows like empty eyes and Chavasse noticed a splash of colour towards the far end.

'What's that?' he said.

'God knows. Cover me and I'll take a look.'

Von Bayern ran through a flower bed, keeping to the shelter of a yew hedge, crossed the terrace and crouched against the wall. Chavasse watched him work his way along to that splash of colour. When he reached it, he paused for a long moment, then raised an arm and beckoned.

Ruth Murray stared up at the sky, her face strangely peaceful in death, the red housecoat spread around her, covering her broken body.

Von Bayern's face was grim. 'He is a butcher, this man.'

Chavasse leaned down to touch the cold cheek. 'I'd say she's been dead for seven or eight hours.'

A French window opened farther along the terrace and as they swung, crouching, Hector Munro appeared, Steiner at his back.

'Where did you find him?' Chavasse said.

'In the courtyard beside the body of his son. And I found Benson, the driver you left with Miss Svensson, in the garage.'

'Dead?'

'I'm afraid so.'

Hector Munro looked his age for the first time since Chavasse had known him, lines of anguish notched deeply into his face, great shoulders bowed in grief.

'What happened, Hector?' Chavasse asked quietly.

There were tears in the old man's eyes. 'He killed my son, Mr. Chavasse—he killed Rory.'

'Who did?'

'Stavrou. He killed Rory and he killed the soldier you left here with the girl.'

'What did he do with her?'

'Took her away to Loch Dubh.'

'To the island?'

'That's right. I followed them. When he came back, he was on his own. I kept out of his way, I had to. God help me, if I could only have laid hands on a gun.'

'Where is he now?'

'That devil Donner arrived maybe twenty minutes ago. They had a deal of conversation in some language strange to me and then they left.'

'Did they go to the loch?'

'They took that direction.'

'The old castle on the island I told you about—Stavrou must have left the girl there and returned to wait for Donner. That's where they'll be.'

'But if Donner's feelings for Miss Svensson are as strong as you say, he's hardly likely to harm her,' von Bayern pointed out

'I wish I could be sure of that.' Chavasse shook his head. 'This is the end of the road for him—he must know that by now. Who can say what a desperate man might do in such circumstances?'

'A good point.' Von Bayern nodded. 'Then it seems we must go into action again.'

'You've done enough—all that anyone could expect—this bit is personal.'

Chavasse turned to move away, there was a quick step behind him, a hand on his shoulder.

Von Bayern sighed. 'I am something of a card player, my friend, and there is one inflexible rule which all good gamblers must obey. Never leave a hand half-played. I have no intention of relaxing that rule now, and, as Sergeant-Major Steiner's superior officer, I can assure you that neither has he. Shall we go?'

It was quiet in the deep hollow there between the hills and the heather seemed to flow down into the loch to be swallowed up by those still black waters. Beyond, through the desolate light of gloaming, the mountains were streaked with orange and a small breeze lifted across the hillside, touching them coldly.

They could see the motor boat moored beside the wooden jetty below the castle wall and Chavasse turned and looked along the shore towards the sandbank from which he had fished a thousand years ago.

'The collapsible boat I mentioned should be somewhere under those bushes.'

They went down through the heather to the shore and Steiner pointed suddenly. 'Look there!'

The boat, or what was left of it, lay on the sand, slashed and torn in a dozen places.

'The Munros,' Chavasse said. 'I might have known.'

'A fine evening for a swim.' Von Bayern looked towards the island. 'Two hundred yards—just about my limit.'

He started to unbutton his military tunic. Chavasse pulled his polo sweater over his head, kicked off his shoes and moved down to the water. Steiner followed him in shirt and pants, his machine pistol slung from his neck.

As von Bayern joined them, Chavasse pointed to the other end of the loch. 'See where the river emerges. There's quite a current. If you can get into the stream of it, you'll be swept in to the island with very little effort.'

'I don't think we should all land at the same place,' von Bayern said. 'It may be useful to come in from different directions.'

Chavasse nodded. 'All right. If Steiner comes in from the other side of the island and you land on the northern tip, I'll make for the jetty and see to the motor boat. That way we'll have him for sure.'

There was nothing more to be said and he walked into the water, catching his breath at the stinging coldness, and struck out in a slow, steady breaststroke that sent gentle ripples coursing across the silvery black surface.

He was strangely calm, trapped in a sort of limbo of the mind, the ancient stronghold on its island rising out of the loch before him, dark against the orange sky, mirrored in the water like some castle in a child's fairy tale.

He swam into the shadow of the walls, a foot touching rounded stones and when he turned, von Bayern's head broke the surface a good fifty yards out. There was no sign of Steiner and Chavasse hurried along the shore, keeping to the bushes, and reached the jetty.

The motor boat floated at its mooring, the engine still warm. He unhooked the painter and pushed it out and a small current took hold, pulling it into deep water. He watched it go, then took the revolver from his hip pocket and went up through the bushes to the arched gateway.

The courtyard was a place of shadows, the battlements stark against a sky that had faded to the colour of molten brass. The tower waited for him, dark and still, no sign of life at all and then a stone rattled underfoot and he crouched, the revolver against his thigh.

There was a movement in the shadows on the stone steps and Steiner appeared on the battlements. He paused warily, his machine pistol ready, then moved on.

As Chavasse reached the top of the steps, Steiner hesitated on the ramparts beside the old cannon, silhouetted against the sky and Stavrou stepped out of the shadow of a buttress behind him. In one smooth movement, the great fist rose and fell, catching Steiner on the nape of the neck, knocking him senseless.

Chavasse moved quickly, the gun coming up and a machine pistol stuttered, bullets spraying the wall beside him, a splinter cutting his cheek.

'All right, sport, let's have it!' Donner called and he moved out of the shadows beside the tower, pushing Asta in front of him.

Remembering von Bayern, Chavasse threw down his revolver and waited as they mounted the battlements. Asta ran forward and he slipped an arm about her shoulders.

'Very touching,' Donner said bitterly.

'You've had it, Donner,' Chavasse said. 'Everything's gone up in smoke. When I left Fhada, Murdoch was even calling in that trawler of yours and there was quite a reception committee waiting.'

Something glowed in Donner's eyes. 'I've still got you, sport. You and her, and that's all that matters in the final analysis.' He laughed harshly. 'You think your boyfriend's pretty hot stuff, don't you, Asta? Well, let's see just how good he is.' He turned to Stavrou who had moved to meet them and said quickly in Russian, 'Break his back for me.'

The great arms swung and Chavasse twisted to duck beneath them and ran for the ramparts. Steiner sprawled face down across his machine pistol. Chavasse tugged at it desperately and as it came free, swung to meet Stavrou who came on like a charging bull.

There was no time to fire. Chavasse swerved and as Stavrou plunged past, smashed him across the back of the skull with the machine pistol. Stavrou cried out in agony and staggered towards the dark line of the wall. He fell to one knee, stood up and turned blindly.

It was the final chance and Chavasse took it, jumping high in the air to deliver that most feared of all *karate* blows, the flying front kick, full in Stavrou's face. He cried out sharply and catapulted back over the wall, down to the rocks below.

Chavasse landed badly on the flagstones, the fall jarring him painfully. As Asta screamed, he turned, pushing himself up on one knee, knowing he was too late, aware only of Donner's face as the machine pistol was raised.

'One moment, Herr Donner!' von Bayern called from the courtyard.

Donner swung in surprise and the German fired three times very fast. The first bullet caught Donner in the shoulder spinning him round, the other two hammered against the wall. He dropped the machine pistol, pushed himself away from the wall with a violent shove and went over the edge into the courtyard.

Chavasse picked himself up and moved to Steiner who groaned and sat up, a dazed expression on his face. 'What happened?'

'A thunderbolt called von Bayern descended, that's what happened,' Chavasse told him.

Asta was at his side and he slipped an arm about her and sagged down on one of the cannon as von Bayern mounted the steps and walked along the ramparts to join them.

In the strange bronze light, he looked indomitable and ageless, the eternal soldier and he leaned on the wall beside them and smiled.

'So, my dear Paul, we live to enjoy our *Oktoberfest* after all?'

Chavasse took a deep, shuddering breath. He was alive, that was all that mattered and he held Asta close, the scent of her warm in his nostrils as the sun finally dipped beyond the mountains and night fell.

CPSIA information can be obtained
at www.ICGtesting.com
Printed in the USA
LVOW01s0041140116
470484LV00026B/721/P